THE CANETERBURY TALES

by

C. J. PAYNE

Published by **CHIMERA**

ISBN 9781780807515

TAMING THERESA
The Private Investigator's Tale

Stenza looked at the desk calendar on his bureau. He read the quote...

"All things come to he who waits."

"What a load of nonsense," he muttered. Then he realised it was the wrong day and pulled off another tiny square to reveal the correct day: Tuesday, 5th February 1952. "Exercise is bunk. If you are healthy, you don't need it: if you are sick you should not take it." Henry Ford.

That was better. Much better. It was quiet at his private detective agency - he'd not had any good cases for a while - he had hoped to stop running the agency from his third floor flat and separate the business from his leisure time but that had proved impossible, so, three years into his new profession, he was still working out of the spacious front room of his London flat. He sighed; his big bulk moved down like a punctured football: he circled a pencil in his hand. He was like a schoolboy waiting to start an exam, a jockey waiting for the off.

He was not sure when he heard the ring on the doorbell, and walked slowly over to his door like a man expecting some post too large to fit in the downstairs tray or some other menial nonsense. He was surprised to answer the door to a thin, tall gentleman wearing a mourning suit.

"Stenza Private Investigations?" The well-spoken gent said, reading from a card. Stenza acknowledged it was and showed him in.

"Take a seat," Stenza said.

"If it's all the same to you I prefer to stand," the man said. Stenza observed that he had a military bearing and stood with his hands behind his back.

"What can I help you with?" Stenza asked.

"Look here, I'll come straight to the point. You've probably heard of me - Lord Hanshaw. Might have seen my photograph in the paper and what not."

Stenza certainly had - not that he had taken any notice of Hanshaw - it was the beautiful raven-haired wife of his who was of more interest to Stenza and to the lens of his daily newspaper, the Daily Record.

"It's about my wife - Lady Theresa Hanshaw - you might have seen her in the paper too."

Stenza certainly had - only the other night she had been photographed arriving at a premier wearing a lovely organza dress; a mink carelessly thrown over her bare shoulder so a touch of flesh was revealed to the earnest hacks and photographers. Lord Hanshaw had certainly struck gold there - a woman half his age that could make a stone head turn.

"Now you mention her I do seem to recall seeing her in the paper," Stenza said laconically.

"As I say, I'll come straight to the point. A chap in the Lords gave me your card and recommended you as a no nonsense sort where discretion is assured. Well, let me say I have a spot of matrimonial bother."

Stenza could well believe it - keeping a beaut like that satisfied was going to be no easy task.

Lord Hanshaw came closer to the desk and Stenza could see an indentation where he wore a monocle.

"You see, I have reason to believe my wife is, how shall I say, carrying on behind my back. Younger chap, bit of a cad, so I believe, caught her attention and won't let go of her - spider and fly - you know how it is?"

Stenza did - matrimonials were the bread and butter of his agency - of most agencies.

"You want me to gather the evidence so you can put it before the divorce courts to stop her claiming half your estate?" Stenza surmised.

For the first time Lord Hanshaw smiled. A tight-lipped, thin smile.

"Not exactly. No." He turned away. "I want you to gather the evidence. I want proof." He turned back. "But I want you to be the one to expose her."

"Me? Why?"

Lord Hanshaw took a gold watch from his waistcoat and glanced at the time as if the whole interview was the utmost bore and he had a train to catch. "I don't expect a fellow like you to understand but I love Lady Theresa and I don't want to divorce her. I don't want this cad to win, do you see? And, I don't want the scandal of being exposed as the cuckolded husband. Wouldn't look good, my position, what?"

"It's a natural enough sentiment - many a man lives with an unfaithful wife."

Hanshaw put away his watch. "Ever read any Shakespeare?"

Stenza laughed. "In my country he was not as popular as he is over here."

"Pity. Read 'A Winter's Tale' - that'll teach you all you need to know about cuckolds."

Stenza found himself absently re-reading the quote on the desk calendar.

"You see old chap," Hanshaw continued. "What I want you to do is get the evidence as you normally would and then find some way of meeting my wife alone and exposing her as an adulterer. Make it clear I put you on the case and say you are going to take the evidence to me. She won't be happy."

Stenza guessed that was something of an understatement.

Hanshaw continued. "She wants to stay with me. So you can tell her that if she wants you to throw the file away, as it were, she will need a lesson. Now what sort of lesson you give her is entirely up to you. You foreign chaps aren't as gentlemanly as us English and would perhaps do things English gentlemen would never do to a lady, if you follow my drift, but that ain't any of mine. You must do what you think fit to get her back to me, thankful and truly grateful that I'm prepared to forgive and forget."

"And what's to stop her Ladyship running down to the Boys in Blue down at Bow Street rather than home to you?" Stenza took a match from a box and lit a cigarette having offered his Lordship one, which had been declined with a wave of his hand.

Again Hanshaw gave a false smile. "Nothing. In theory. In reality what would she gain if she revealed she took a hiding, if that's what it's to be, from a grubby little man in a backstreet private eye business that had proof of her adulterous relationship? As I say, she wants to stay with me, she doesn't want a divorce and if she reveals anything she knows she'll be in court faster than a hare on heat."

Stenza exhaled a long stream of smoke. "And you don't fancy teaching your good lady wife a lesson yourself? It's what most men do with an errant wife; things are best sorted out in the family home."

"Look Stenza, you ain't English so you don't understand the upper classes. We don't like to get our hands dirty. We give orders and we expect them to be followed, do you hear? We don't go around flogging our wives as if they were Etonian wags, what? Now, all I'm saying is that if you think Lady Theresa deserves a lesson then so be it, but as far as I'm concerned I've asked for nothing more than an investigation into my wife's comings and goings, is that clear?"

Stenza said it was.

"And you'll be well reward," Hanshaw continued. He threw some money on the desk.

"That's expenses; I'll pay you double on completion. As I say, all I want is my wife back begging for forgiveness and vowing not to cheat on me again. Clear?"

"As crystal. I just need a few details about the good Lady Theresa."

Hanshaw at last sat down. "Well she's a young 'un - only twenty-five. You've seen the photographs in the paper but I brought these."

He reached into his inside pocket and produced an envelope. Stenza placed the contents on his desk - photos of the young bride in a bikini, in evening dress and a head shot - Stenza wondered, not for the first time, if there was something underhand about the assignment - that perhaps Hanshaw found the whole thing erotically charged. Maybe he even enjoyed the thought of his wife with another man - some men did. Or maybe he enjoyed the thought of his wife being punished by another man.

Stenza placed the photos in his drawer and counted the money Hanshaw had thrown down. There was enough to cover the expenses for ten assignments. At last he took up his sharpened pencil.

"Now, down to the nitty-gritty," Stenza said. "Where does she go? And who do you think she is meeting?"

"The cad's name is Clayton - he's about the same age. Old Etonian. Pleasure seeker. Bets on horses and likes cards. Bit of a rascal." Hanshaw went on to list Lady Theresa's favourite activities and where Stenza might find her. "How long do you think it'll take?" he concluded.

Stenza shrugged. "Who can say? But someone as high profile as your wife - well, it shouldn't take long."

It didn't. Within a couple of weeks Stenza had all the evidence any husband would need to prove infidelity and file for divorce - theatre tickets, details of hotel rooms, train tickets carelessly discarded. He had found out that her lover, Earnest Clayton, was also carrying on with another married woman.

Stenza even photographed Lady Theresa and Clayton together - covertly of course. The fact that Lady Theresa was so popular with the press was a massive asset as he had been able to use his fake press pass to gain access to a theatre and a symphony hall and photograph her Ladyship with her lover. Resplendent in a lavish evening dress. There was nothing shy about Lady Theresa, who liked to flaunt her natural assets - not to mention those bestowed on her by her loving husband. Throughout the assignment Stenza could only think of Hanshaw's somewhat bizarre demand that he be the one that punished her. Stenza had to admit that his heart started to beat with a growing passion whenever he saw Lady Theresa - the idea of teaching her a lesson, well, that was something he was only too happy to oblige with, but how? And how to lure her to his flat?

In the middle of the third week he phoned his Lordship and informed him that he had the evidence.

"Well, you know what to do, get on with it!" his Lordship said tersely.

Stenza had been hoping for some direction; instead it was left to him to come up with a suitable punishment for an errant young wife.

At last he planned his operation. He would see Lady Theresa as Hanshaw had suggested and tell her he had the evidence of an affair. He would then blackmail her and pretend that he needed money from her not to pass the evidence on to Hanshaw.

An opportunity arose whilst her Ladyship was out shopping. She was wearing a tight-fitting suit and high heels and a limousine, driven by a chauffeur, crept along the pavement beside her as she made purchases. One thing Stenza had noticed about her Ladyship was that she was rarely on her own. He approached her in the street.

"Lady Therese Hanshaw?"

"Yes."

Stenza wafted her perfume and eyed the expensive mink.

"Can I have a word in private?"

"What's it about?"

"Your husband." Stenza paused. "And your lover."

"Walsh - pull over for a minute and take a walk. I just need to have a word with this man in the confines of the Bentley."

Walsh duly obliged by opening the door for them both before drifting off down the High Street.

"Well?" Lady Theresa said sharply. "I'm not accustomed to being accosted in the street."

Stenza ignored her. "Lord Hanshaw has asked me to compile a dossier on your relationship with Viscount Clayton, which I have now done and I'm about to show to his Lordship."

"Well, show it to him, why should I care?"

This was not the response Stenza had expected or wanted.

"The thing is, your Ladyship; I'm prepared not to show it to him for a small consideration. I have a large brown envelope with photographs, train tickets, details from hotel stays, in my office desk, and I'm prepared to let you have them for a small fee, and then inform your husband that I've not managed to trace any wrongdoing on your part."

"Get lost! You mean-spirited blackmailer. I'll not be party to such a lowdown scam. If you have evidence show my husband and be damned. Now get out of my car before I call the police."

Stenza was stunned. He pressed the door lever to get out of the car. "Here is my card - if you wish to discuss the matter with me. I'll give you three days before I reveal my hand to his Lordship. Good day, my Lady."

With that Stenza left the car rather shaken by his encounter.

Stenza had another smaller assignment to occupy his time and tried to forget about Lord and Lady Hanshaw's matrimonial problems - he had decided on a course of action and bought implements in readiness, but required her Ladyship to take the bait, which she did not seem prepared to do... maybe his Lordship had misjudged his wife and she was happy for all to be revealed.

On the third day he was preparing to contact Lord Hanshaw to inform of the ill-fated assignment. When he got back to his flat late in the evening, having dined out with friends, he found that the room had been disturbed. He made a quick scan of his desk but nothing appeared to have been touched. He took off his jacket and went to the bathroom to run a bath, and it was then that he smelt perfume. Expensive perfume.

His attention was caught by a movement behind a curtain. He walked quickly to it and drew it back with a sharp rip. There, in all her finery, was Lady Hanshaw. Stenza grabbed her by the hand and pulled her into the room.

"What the hell are you doing here?" he shouted, genuinely annoyed.

"I'm sorry. I told the hall concierge I was your sister and I had some very important news. He said you were at dinner so I asked him to let me in so I could wait - I said mummy was ill. I've been to the theatre but left during the interval saying I was unwell."

Stenza took in the lovely dress with a full bodice; it was strapless and revealed her Ladyship's ample bust, which rose and fell heavily. Suddenly, Stenza felt an extraordinary sense of power.

"What the hell are you doing, coming to my flat without permission?" he said with mock rage.

"I... I... I," she stuttered.

"You what?"

"Wanted the envelope with the evidence. You can't let my husband see it. That would be so beastly."

"You shouldn't have had an affair then, should you?" Stenza felt like slapping her. After all, wasn't that what Lord Hanshaw had wanted?

"Please let me have that envelope - I'll pay for it. Please, just don't tell my husband, please."

Her large brown eyes beseeched Stenza, pleaded as only a beautiful woman can.

Stenza thought fast. "Who knows you're here?"

"No one. The friends I was with think I've gone home to my husband. I took a cab tonight rather than the chauffeur so no one has seen me come here."

Providence had landed him the perfect catch. Maybe the first calendar motto was right after all - *all good things come to those who wait*. And this was certainly a good thing, a very good thing. He suddenly realised he was still holding her wrist. He gave a sharp tug and she stumbled uneasily on her high heels.

"Look, Lady Theresa, I've been employed by your husband to investigate your affair and give him the evidence. What he does with it is his business. He is my client. I gave you a way out but you threw it back in my face. You have admitted, in this room, that you came here to steal that information and that is now a criminal matter."

"Please don't involve the police."

"I'm going to have to..."

"I'll deny it - no one would believe the word of a common little pipsqueak like you over a Lady."

Stenza smiled. "I'm afraid your Ladyship is wrong. For unfortunately this room is bugged. I use it as an office and all conversations that take place in here are recorded," he lied.

Her Ladyship blanched. "You wouldn't do that, you wouldn't be so mean!"

"Wouldn't I?"

Lady Theresa pulled at her wrist. "Let me go! I've had enough of this. You're a beastly man. I want to go home."

Stenza released her wrist. "Your Ladyship is free to go, but there is a slight possibility that I may be able to come up with a solution to our problem, and that solution would disappear as soon as you left the room."

"What on earth can you mean?" she said earnestly.

"Well, my Lady, I need time to think, and I think better in the bath, which is what I was going to have before I realised I had a burglar in my flat. If your Ladyship would remain here, while I have a bath, I may be able to think through a few solutions. At present you are in an almighty fix - you have attempted to steal from my flat using subterfuge as a means of entry and you have cheated on your husband."

Her Ladyship bowed her head. "Don't involve the police," she repeated. "I could not bear the scandal."

Stenza pulled out one of his dining room chairs and placed it in the middle of the floor.

"Sit down."

Her Ladyship did not move.

Stenza raised his voice. "I said sit down!"

This time she obediently lifted her skirts around her legs and sat on the chair.

"Now, I'm going to take a bath while I think about the best way to resolve this situation to everyone's satisfaction, and while I take my bath I want you to sit there. Agreed?"

"Agreed," her Ladyship said.

"And, as you have already said you might leave, you will allow me to use a little restraint."

Lady Theresa looked around, her face ashen. "Whatever do you mean, Mr Stenza?"

"I mean I'm going to tie you up."

"You can't... you wouldn't... dare..."

"Oh wouldn't I? If you don't wish to obey me then leave now and I'll show the brown envelope to your husband and you can take your chances in the divorce courts."

Her Ladyship made no movement bar tucking her hands beneath her skirts. Stenza knew she had accepted her fate. He moved behind the chair and roughly grabbed her arms and pulled them through the back of it. He then tied her wrists expertly. Next, he tied a thin rope around her slim ankles, tying each to a leg of the chair and, for good measure, a piece of rope around her waist. When Lady Theresa was well and truly moored to the chair he walked to his record player.

"I'm a big fan of Shostakovich - do you have any preferences in the classical music department?"

"No, just hurry up and have your damned bath and release me from this ghastly ordeal."

Stenza smiled. "I never hurry a bath; in fact with everything going on I've forgotten to run the thing."

He marched smartly to the bathroom and turned on the taps, and soon the sound of gushing water filled the flat.

Stenza went back to the player and drew out records, inspecting each for scratches.

He was proud of his collection and always bought a new recording whenever he could. At last he settled on Tchaikovsky and placed the needle on the LP.

He came back to his victim. She sat in the chair so delicately, her breasts heaving in the bodice of her white strapless dress. She was so enticing, so sexy, no wonder Lord Hanshaw was so smitten with her. Any man would love to have such a beautiful wife.

"Now, are you going to be quiet or do I need to gag you?" Stenza asked.

"I'll be quiet... but you'll pay for this you... you monster..."

He cut her a blow across the face. It was a quick slap - hard and fast and painful. He had used it on many a man... and the occasional woman.

Lady Theresa looked up, tears and fear in her eyes.

"I'm sorry," she said. "I know you're only doing your job... it's my husband I should save my wrath for."

"Don't let it happen again," Stenza said. He went to the bathroom, and while he lay luxuriating in the soapy warmth he thought about his victim tied to the chair. Lady Theresa had certainly learnt a salutary lesson and he hoped Lord Hanshaw would be pleased with him. He doubted she would be unfaithful again. He slowly got out of the bath and dressed, and then returned to the lounge.

"Still here?" he joked, pouring himself a drink.

Lady Theresa didn't answer.

"I'll dispose of the evidence of you having an affair and tell your husband I could find none of infidelity," Stenza started. "Obviously, Lord Hanshaw knows you have been seeing this cad Clayton, so when I've finished with you tonight I will take you home, and I expect you to confess that you were smitten by Clayton but you never actually had an affair and that you've finished with him. Throw yourself on your husband's mercy and beg him for forgiveness. We both know he will forgive you, so he doesn't need to know you had an affair."

The record finished and Stenza took the needle off and carefully removed the record and placed it back in its sleeve. "You'll need to write a letter to Clayton tonight telling him it's all over, and I'll post it."

"And what do you want in return?" Lady Theresa asked.

"I want to spank you," Stenza said calmly. The words sent a warm shiver tingling through his body.

She gaped, shocked.

"You want to *what?*"

Stenza was more forceful. "After I've released you, and you've written to Clayton, I'm going to spank you before I take you home."

"But that's... that's... too much. I'll give you the diamond necklace I'm wearing, my wrist watch - anything."

"I do not seek material wealth, your Ladyship. I seek justice. Your husband may be a fool but he dotes on you and does not see you as the flirtatious coquette you are. He has lavished goods on you and in return you have betrayed him. Even now he wants you back. Giving me jewels, which are a mere trifle to you, is no form of punishment; you need, you deserve, a proper punishment."

"But I..."

"They're my terms... take them or leave them."

She had no choice, Stenza knew that, so when he'd released her and he had the "Dear John" letter to Clayton safely tucked in his jacket pocket he pulled Lady

Theresa by the wrist back to the chair she had spent the last hour or more tied to. This time it was Stenza who sat on it. With a violent jerk he pulled Lady Theresa over his knee. His right hand delved beneath the thick net petticoats of her dress. He pushed up the material until his hand felt the porcelain buttocks. Lovely silk French knickers covered the blooming orbs, and with one tear he pulled them down to reveal the loveliest plump posterior he had ever seen in his life. The upper classes certainly had fine backsides, Stenza mused. It was almost too perfect to spank, but the urging of his cock told him he had a job to do which would give him as much pleasure as it did Lord Hanshaw. He brought his hand up and then down with a thunderous smack. The first, on a pure white backside, was always the most pleasurable, Stenza believed. Seeing the flesh quickly redden, seeing the backside muscles twitch as the victim whined and took in a sharp intake of breath - that was pure undiluted pleasure. Stenza spanked her again.

"No!" Lady Theresa exclaimed. "You bully, I won't have it."

"It's this or that envelope's going to your husband," Stenza remained her. He brought his hand down for a third time. Flesh impacted on flesh. The left buttock was squashed under the power of the blow. Lady Theresa breathed uneasily. Stanza was a long way from the finishing line. He had given her three nursery smacks, left buttock, right buttock, left buttock, to get his eye in; now he shifted on the chair and moved Lady Theresa further over his knee so he had a good aim and angle. Her pretty little head was resting on the carpet, her dark hair fell about her, her hands tried to grip the floor covering. When Stenza was in position he was ready to tan Lady Theresa's backside harder than it had ever been tanned before - or was likely to be again - unless Lord Hanshaw deemed it necessary to again give him such a satisfying job.

Stenza went to work beating out a tattoo, left check, right check. Hard, fast smacks; not raising his right hand too high but reserving his energy for a sustained spanking which would leave the buttocks red and sore for days. No quick hard smack here, but a deep throbbing pain - that was the answer. And Stanza was an expert. Oh, plenty of female clients had found his way over his knee, not to mention female criminals when he had worked for the police in his native Italy. Stenza often found that a spanking was the most effective and quickest way to correct an errant criminal, and he was sure that Lady Theresa would not cheat on Lord Hanshaw again.

He brought his hand down again and again. Lady Theresa yelped and yelled and swore and moaned and cried and beseeched him to stop, but Stenza was oblivious to such pleas. She deserved a spanking and she was going to get a spanking.

Lady Theresa spent a full ten minutes resting across his lap receiving the hardest and longest spanking she had ever received in her life. When she got back on her high-heeled feet her mascara had run, her eyes were blotchy with crying and her neat dress was dishevelled - and her cheeks (all four of them) were crimson: in short she looked a complete mess.

She stood in the living room panting. "You beast," she cried. "How could you?"

"Very easily and I'll do it again if you cheat on Lord Hanshaw."

Lady Theresa tried to pull down her dress. "You're not a gentleman you're an animal."

Stanza laughed heartily. "I think your husband has much the same view. Perhaps that's why he employed me. Seems I have something of a reputation. Still, if it gets the job done then I'm satisfied."

9

Stenza's cock was fit to burst and he was dying to relieve himself. Fortunately Lady Theresa's skirt had masked his erection. She grabbed her small clutch bag from the side and hurried to the bathroom. He knew she would be some time so he unleashed his manhood and gave his large cock a few jerks, so turned on he came quickly. The thought of Lady Theresa over his knee was going to provide an erotic fantasy for many years to come, he knew that.

When Lady Theresa emerged from the bathroom, refreshed but still red-eyed (and Stenza knew, red-bottomed) he offered to take her home. Without saying a word she took her fur stole from the back of a chair and breezed out of the flat, wafting perfume and rustling skirts. He grinned; she was certainly an unhappy young lady.

On the way back to Lord Hanshaw's home Stenza stopped by a post box and posted the letter she had written to Clayton. That infatuation was well and truly over.

He drew up outside Lord Hanshaw's London residence, and Lady Theresa got out of the car without saying a word.

"Remember what you have to do," he said.

"I am not a child, though you treat me like one," she snapped. "I'll tell my husband I had a brief flirtation with Viscount Clayton, nothing more, and hope he forgives me my indiscretion."

"And I'll dispose of the evidence and tell him I could find no proof of an affair," Stenza said, though he had already decided to keep one or two photographs of her for his personal use.

Lady Theresa slammed the car door and walked up the drive to the white Georgian townhouse. A few minutes later a butler ushered her in and Lady Theresa, resplendent with spanked backside, disappeared from Stanza's life.

"My word, you did a mighty fine job there, Stenza," Lord Hanshaw said a few days later. This time he collapsed into a chair. "I don't need to know the finer details but I know my wife was suitably chastised, what?"

Stenza agreed that she had been.

Lord Hanshaw lit a cigar. "She confessed to an infatuation with Clayton which we both know to be a lie, but that's bye the bye. She begged for forgiveness and that's all I wanted. She told me she had finished with him and written to tell him it was over. I suspect you were behind that?"

Stenza confirmed he was.

"Whatever you have done to her has made her awfully obsequious; she can't do enough for me these days, and that includes in the bedroom, what. No wonder you have such a good reputation in the Upper House. If you weren't a foreign national I'd put your name forward for a knighthood. Damn well deserve one."

Stenza leaned across his desk. "I do not need any honours; my work is its own reward, Lord Hanshaw."

"That and money, of course." Lord Hanshaw stood up and went to his pocket and took out an envelope. "There's the rest of my fee. Never has money been better spent. Well cheerio, and thanks awfully for all you've done."

Stenza watched as Lord Hanshaw shut the door behind him. There was definitely a spring in his step. Once again he was a happily married man.

SPANKER BANKER

The Banker's Tale

George Davies loved being a bank manager. He loved the power. He loved being a respected man about town but most of all he loved the female staff. Women, George often considered, were better than men at customer service, and since he had resorted to an unofficial policy of only recruiting women to work behind the cash desk he had seen his customers increase. Head office was happy and asked him how he did it. Perhaps they could learn a trick or two to transfer to other banks. George was circumspect; it was just good customer service and word of mouth. Even so, George knew he had hit on a winning formula for, despite women's lib, it was still mainly men who held the purse strings and decided what bank to invest with and where to obtain a mortgage.

Gradually he had started to expand his policy. At first he just employed women and then, as some had left to have children, he started to employ pretty young women - again, he noticed a spike in his customers. George was very satisfied, especially as he also saved money as he did not have to pay them the same as men. Indeed, the only other male member of staff was his deputy... well, a female bank manager would never do.

It was 1968 and London was swinging - but not that much swinging had reached the outskirts of Surbiton, George considered. Still, he loved the Sixties, not so much for the music which he thought of as nothing more than an awful row, but for the fashions - particularly the fashions that young ladies wore. The skirts and dresses seemed to get shorter every year and he liked the fashion for PVC boots and high heels. He was in his fifties, married and had two grown up sons, but that did not stop him looking, did it?

Not that he just looked. One thing George liked about his young cashiers was that they were more than open to a bit of slap and tickle. And so, when he said goodbye to his wife, Meredith, in the morning and walked out of the front door, his bowler hat on his head and his rolled up umbrella in his hand - the epitome of middle-class respectability - George was often thinking about "his girls", as he called them, and wondering whether or not he would get an opportunity to release his infamous Wandering Hand.

He knew some people would think of him as a dirty old man, but as far as he was concerned just because he was fifty-five did not mean he didn't still have yearnings, and the young women who worked in the bank - well, they just made it all worthwhile.

Only the day before Nicola had come in to his office having typed some letters. She had been wearing a very short floral-print dress with puff sleeves and a high neck. She stood by his desk and placed the letters in front of him. George liked to inspect things thoroughly. He was a stickler for grammar, spelling and punctuation and knew he would have to circle at least three words with his pencil; it would probably take Nicola two attempts to get the letters right. George finished reading, and had only made one correction.

"Good," he had said, and placed the pencil down on the blotter. "Let's have a look at this one, shall we?"

As the words left his lips he slapped Nicola playfully on the back of her bare leg. She blushed and held her hands tightly in front of her. Then, George had let his arm drop to the side of his chair, and started to move it up, under the hem of her skirt. He started to feel her knickers as his cock hardened in his trousers. He memorised a couple of mistakes; his right hand too engrossed to pick up the pencil. Nicola had not say a word as George's hand roamed around for a while, so he'd given her buttock a nice squeeze. He watched as she looked awkward and tried to move away, clearly conscious that she should not make a fuss. Finally, he withdrew his hand and marked the mistakes.

"There you go now, run along and correct those, there's still time to get them in the post."

"Yes, Mr Davies," Nicola had said, and left the office hurriedly. George picked up the phone on his desk and dialled an outside line.

"Sorry dear," he had said, "I'll be slightly late home tonight. I've been tied up at the bank."

He had listened to Meredith nag him for a while.

"I know we promised to go around to the Ambrose-Daytons, but that can't be helped, commerce calls."

He had put the phone down. "Silly woman," he muttered. Then he thought of Nicola back out in the main office, no doubt telling the other women about her encounter with Mr Davies' Wandering Hand. He knew they all joked about it - he'd had it for years and it almost had a character and life of its own. It was a bit like a ventriloquist's dummy. The Wandering Hand. He smiled. Hopefully he would get another feel of Nicola's pert arse when she came in for him to sign the letters.

And his luck was in. It was Nicola who came back with the letters, and again Nicola had received the wandering hand treatment. George liked how she stood up straight when he fondled her, how she held her hands together tightly, how she smiled falsely as if she was enjoying the experience, and most of all how she continued to act in a professional way as if he wasn't really touching her up. When the bank closed, and the rest of the staff had gone home, George went to the gents and undid his trousers. He always liked the end of the day; the part where he sat on the toilet and relived all his fondling activities. On this occasion it had only been Nicola, but on some days he might fondle two or three girls.

His activities always followed a pattern. First, with a new girl, he would complement them on something, like an item of dress. Then it would be anatomy - "You have lovely blue eyes." Then it may be a quip - "Not wearing a bra today?" Or, "You've certainly got a pert backside when you bend over." From there it would be a slap if they leant too far over the filing cabinets, or maybe a pinch if he got behind them in the corridor. Wandering Hand didn't come out till much later. That was the final piece in the jigsaw; once a girl was comfortable with his innuendo and touching Wandering Hand would come out. Wandering Hand would always start over clothes and, after a couple of successful missions, he would let it loose and it would crawl under a skirt, or make a play for breasts, though this was often reserved for the Christmas party season. Still more than a few bosoms had been brushed, tweaked or fondled in his office - and not just staff breasts either.

George knew he was helped by his reputation. All the women who worked for him were quickly briefed by more experienced members of staff to expect a visit from Wandering Hand, and George knew that was half the battle won; by giving warnings to their colleagues that he liked a fondle they actually made his life easier. When a girl came to his office she knew she was likely to get touched - that meant, over the years, George had often dispensed with his tried and tested procedure and now went straight for the outer bum grope before moving under the skirt on the next occasion. After all, it was what was expected of him.

What George liked was that a number of his customers knew about him as well. Of course the cashiers all had families and friends and most lived locally, and then there were the girls who got married and left but remained customers of the bank. George found there were quite a number of mature women who would openly flirt with him and liked nothing more than a bum tweak or a breast fondle in his office. Also, George had moved the two chairs where customers sat from behind his desk to beside his desk. This meant when a man and wife entered his office the man would often let the woman sit down first and she would sit by George, and this provided him with the opportunity to look at long stretches of often bare legs. He loved the way women tried to tug their miniskirts down when he looked at them, as if they could miraculously develop more material. It was amazing how oblivious most men were to George's ploy - the women never were.

His fondling activity had led to numerous affairs. His wife knew, hence her irritation whenever he said he was working late. To her it was just code for "I'm having an affair" - even though most times he worked late he found himself alone in the toilet cubicle pulling his trunk for all it was worth and thinking about the day's fondling.

That Thursday morning George arrived at the bank to find a blonde beauty waiting for him.

"This is Gemma," Nicola said. "She's our latest recruit."

George cursed. He had forgotten all about her. He had taken her on as general help when she had come in looking for work, and then forgotten about it. She had been visiting her Aunt in Surbiton and was desperate to stay as she'd not wanted to miss out on "swinging London", which was where it was all "happening, man!" George hated that slovenly Americanised drawl by feckless goons who called themselves "singers". Still, what was he to do with Gemma?

"Show her a few ropes, Nicola, while I sort myself out, and then I'll call her in."

"Yes, Mr Davies."

George went to his office and organised himself for the day, then sat thinking about Gemma. From what he remembered she had no qualifications or experience in banking, and he had only offered her a job because he'd been taken in by her lovely Emerald Isle eyes and her long, baby-blonde hair which framed the sweetest face he had ever seen. After a few minutes he called her into his office.

"Take a seat, Miss O'Leary," he said.

She ran her hands under the tight black, knee-length skirt and sat down carefully.

"I'm afraid there's been a misunderstanding," he began. "We can't employ you at present - there are no spare jobs and you're not trained to work as a cashier."

Gemma burst into tears. George had not expected that reaction.

"But you said you had a job for me!" she sobbed.

"I thought I did."

"I've been back to Dublin and collected all my things and come to live with my Aunt."

George smiled. You should have got it in writing, then it would be binding, he thought. Still, he felt a little sorry for the girl.

"How old are you?" he asked.

"Eighteen."

"And you've come all the way from Dublin to Surbiton to live with your Aunt so you can work in a bank?"

She nodded her head.

"That's a big thing for someone as young and pretty as you to do," George said.

Gemma smiled through her tears. "I'll do anything," she said. "Only I want to be near London so I can go to discotheques and meet the Beatles and the Stones and have a really groovy time. I just love music. Do you dig music, Sir?"

"Yes, but probably not the same kind as you."

"Will you give me a job, Sir?"

"Listen, Gemma, as you've come all the way from Dublin to work here I think the least I can do is take you on a month's trial, is that fair?"

"Oh, thank you, Sir."

"You can start by making me a nice hot cup of tea. Nicola will show you where the kitchen is and how to prepare it. I'm very particular about my tea. I'm not one of these that drink that awful coffee - dirty American habit that is."

"I will, Sir, thank you again. You've been very kind, so you have."

George watched as Gemma's backside wriggle out of the office. I'll be kind to that arse as well if I get half a chance, he thought.

Two weeks later he happened to walk past some girls on their lunch break. They were busy reading pop magazines and talking about a "dishy" new pop star and saying how they "dug" one of the latest LPs. George took some letters over to another desk and casually observed the three girls: Sarah, Gemma and Nicola. He was pleased that Gemma had followed her colleagues and now wore miniskirts to work, which showed her lovely long legs to best advantage. He knew she would soon be ripe for Wandering Hand. As he walked back to his office he passed close by and overheard a conversation which made his ears prick up.

"I came home late from a discotheque on Saturday and missed the bus, and my Aunt had a right go at me. She's just not with it."

"Is she strict, your Aunt?" Sarah, one of the cashiers, asked.

"Oh ha," Gemma said, eating celery. "She's threatened me with the belt before, and on Saturday she slapped my face because I answered her back."

"I wouldn't stand for that," Nicola said. "You're eighteen and you can do what you want. No adult can to tell you what to do."

"I wouldn't have any square tell me what to do," Sarah agreed. "She's just jealous because you're young and hip."

"It's how things are in Ireland," Gemma said. "Parents are stricter."

"Yeah, but you're not in Ireland now are you, you're in London. Well, Surbiton." They all laughed.

"What do you think, Mr Davies?" Sarah asked as he passed by.

"Sorry, Sarah, I wasn't listening."

"Gemma here was just saying how her Aunt slapped her because she came in late. What do you think?"

He knew the girls were taking the rise out of him, like naughty school kids with a strict teacher.

"I think Gemma's Aunt is right. Gemma knows the house rules, don't you Gemma?"

Gemma nodded.

"Therefore, if Gemma chooses to disobey them then she should be punished."

"But her Aunt slapped her face, Mr Davies," Nicola interjected.

"But did it teach you a lesson, Gemma?"

Gemma agreed that it had.

"I rest my case," George said, and walked back to his office.

Later, when Gemma brought in his afternoon tea, he introduced her to Wandering Hand. He circled around her cotton miniskirt and then went for the hem. His fingertips quickly moved under her skirt and touched her knickers.

"So, your Aunt's strict, is she?" he asked as she recoiled from his touch.

"Yes, Mr Davies."

"And what else has she threatened to do apart from slap you and threaten you with a belt?"

George's cock was beating against his zipper. He loved the way Gemma blushed to the roots of her blonde hair, how she spilt the tea as she slid the tray onto his desk with nervous, shaking hands.

"She's threatened to send me home," she said innocently.

"But punishments, what punishments has she threatened you with?" George asked impatiently.

Her bum twitched nervously as his hand made small circular motions across her knickers. He was sure the other girls would have told her about his Wandering Hand and she would have half expected it; certainly she was taking it in good faith, but then she did not want to go home to Dublin.

"She says mum - her sister - didn't spank me nearly enough as a child and if she had been my mum she would have spanked me twice as hard and thrice as often, but she's not got any children being as she's not married, so she's not."

George's hand continued to circle. "But you obviously like your Aunt as you wouldn't have moved in with her, would you?"

"I was desperate to be near London, Mr Davies," Gemma said. "I'll move out to a bedsit, so I will, when I've saved enough money. I don't want to live with a square all my life."

The tray was down in front of him. Tea had slopped everywhere and it was far too weak. Why was it she could not even make a decent cup of tea?

"Gemma, I think you need to show a bit more respect for your Aunt. She has lived in the world a lot longer than you and she knows a lot more than you. She sets the rules while you live in her house. Now, when you go home tonight I want you to tell her that Mr Davies has said that if there is any more disobedience by you at home he'll deal with you at work. In fact, better still, I'll write a letter to her to that effect. Now, what's her name?"

"Miss Brady, Mr Davies."

George removed his hand from beneath her skirt and gave her bum a smack. She released a little cry and left the office.

That Aunt, he thought, was a woman after his own heart. He took up a pen and some paper and started to write.

Dear Miss Brady,

As you are aware your niece is working at this bank on a monthly basis, filing and making tea. She says she wants to be near London and that she is staying with you until she can afford a bedsit, on her own or with friends. I overheard her telling colleagues that you'd had to admonish her on Saturday for staying out late, so when she brought my tea in this afternoon I told her that she should follow your instructions while she lives under your roof, and it was correct and proper for you to punish her in any way you thought suitable. Please forgive this intrusion into your family life, but I must admit I was incensed by the conversation the cashiers were having, generally talking in a disrespectful tone. Therefore, with your written permission, I would like to punish Gemma, not for any work misdeeds, which I feel would be inappropriate as the bank has a clear procedure for removing errant members of staff and Gemma is only here temporarily, but if she again talks of you in a disrespectful way or I discover you have had occasion to punish her and she has not heeded the lesson. In short, I look to be a support in the workplace for your parental guidance. Once again, please forgive my intrusion and ignore my request if you feel it lacks merit.

Once written, George folded the letter carefully and placed it in a manila envelope. At the end of the day he called Gemma into his office and gave it to her.

"Take this to your Aunt," he ordered. He knew she would as she was actually very deferential to authority, though she liked to act as if she wasn't. It was part of being young and "trendy", George knew that.

The next day she handed him a letter. He casually placed it on his desk as if he was not interested. Later he placed it in a drawer; he would wait until lunchtime before reading it.

He worked steadily through the morning, seeing a customer and sorting out some enquiries, and then he went to his drawer and pulled out the letter. The writing was neat. He took a letter knife and opened it. He quickly looked at the contents. The letter contained an address at the top of the page.

Dear Mr Davies,

Thank you for your kind letter.

If you overhear my niece talking in a disrespectful way about me in future you are quite at liberty to punish her in any way you think fit. However, I would appreciate it if you would telephone me on an individual basis should such indiscretions occur so I can give my verbal permission before you proceed.

I thank you for your invaluable support. It is very difficult to enforce discipline in the current climate where respect for authority seems to have crumbled.

Yours faithfully,

Eileen Brady.

George pulled out his writing paper and penned a reply, thanking her for her letter and informing her that, of course, he would phone for verbal permission before proceeding to any punishment of Gemma. He posted that letter rather than pass it to Gemma. It was then just a question of waiting.

Over the coming weeks George found himself listening in on conversations that the girls had in the outer office, but alas Gemma neither failed to report any further indiscretions nor said anything derogatory about her Aunt. He renewed her contract for another month and waited... and waited. At first the idea of spanking Gemma - if indeed Miss Brady allowed him to do it - had filled his fantasies, but he felt the moment had passed, and that, for whatever reason, things had settled down between Gemma and her Aunt and she was perhaps not quite so disobedient. Then, one day he was in the toilet when he heard a cashier sobbing in the ladies' toilet next door. There was a grate between the two rooms which meant every word could be heard if people were so indiscreet as to chat in there rather than go back to work. In fact, George often lurked in the toilet to find out information about female members of staff and to hear exaggerated erection-rising reports of his Wandering Hand. It was not long before the toilet door opened and a new girl came in.

"What's up, Gem?" It was Nicola.

"It's my Aunt," Gemma sobbed. "She's such a bloody battleaxe, so she is. She won't let me do anything, the old dragon. She's stopped me going to discotheques and I met a nice boy but she would not let me date him."

"Poor you. Why don't you just move out?"

"I can't afford it. I never realised how expensive it is in London," Gemma cried.

"Well, you'll just have to have it out with her. Tell her to get with it and stop acting like a square."

"I can't, things have got a lot worse since Mr Davies wrote to her. I don't know what he said but she keeps saying if I misbehave she'll tell him and he'll deal with me, and then I bet I lose my job, wouldn't you know? That's why I never say anything at work; I don't want Mr Davies ear-wigging. That man is such a creep, he makes my skin crawl."

"You think Mr Davies said he would sack you?" Nicola said with genuine surprise.

"I'm sure he did! Aunty uses it as a threat against me all the time, and it's just fab working here and being with all the girls and knowing I'm so close to where there's so many happenings; I don't want to leave," she sobbed.

George heard a rustling of skirts and Nicola comforting her and telling her everything would be all right, and soon there would be a revolution and all the nasty old squares like Mr Davies and her Aunt would be replaced by hip youngsters who dug music and liked to hang out. Things would be different when the young ruled the world.

George looked at his watch; no wonder no one gets any work done round here, he thought, and marched back to his office.

He had heard enough. Quite enough. Later that afternoon, when the office was quite, he phoned Miss Brady and repeated the conversation he had overheard in the toilet. He did not even need to embellish it. Poor Gemma had hung herself with her own words, he knew that.

"What do you intend to do, Mr Davies?" Miss Brady asked. "Is she going to lose her

17

job?"

George felt his cock rise - it obviously wanted to hear the answer too. The phone felt sweaty in his palm and started to shake, yet he knew he had to say the answer in a mater-of-fact way.

"Gemma is not going to lose her job, Miss Brady. As I made clear in my letter I do not feel that her personal life should interfere with her working life. She is actually a jolly good worker when she's not crying in the toilet. No, Miss Brady, I'm going to spank her."

He let the words whistle down the electronic line. There was silence. His cock was pulsing. His heart thumped.

"Do you think you should? I mean, you're not going to get in trouble with your bank, are you? I would hate it if you were to get in trouble for my sake, so I would," Eileen Brady fretted.

George released a satisfied sigh. "Look Miss Brady, this is a private matter. It'll happen tonight after work, after the bank is closed. No one will ever know apart from me, you and Gemma. If you wish you are quite at liberty to walk to the bank at five o'clock and watch proceedings."

"Mr Davies, if you don't mind I think I would rather you just got on with it. I do appreciate all your kindness to me and your support, but perhaps if you could just mend Gemma's ways without the need for me to be involved, I would be eternally grateful, so I would."

After he put the phone down George stood up and looked out of the window. The back of the bank looked out onto a park and he could see mothers with silver cross prams and suited businessmen walking to appointments. It was a glorious sunny day and he had never felt so happy. He called Meredith and told her he would be late home, this time quite rude to her when she questioned him about what he was doing, and he ended the conversation by slamming the phone down on her. Why should he care for her stupid concerns about his fidelity?

When Gemma came in with his afternoon tea tray he told her bluntly that he wanted to see her at five p.m. and he was going to have a serious word with her. He wanted her to feel uneasy for the rest of the afternoon.

At five, as the rest of the staff left and the bank closed up for the day, Gemma knocked on his office door and came in. He told her to stand in front of his desk. He had written down some of the things he had overheard Gemma say and he repeated them to her. Her mouth dropped open and she looked aghast.

"I'm sorry, Mr Davies," she said. "Please don't tell my Aunt."

"I already have, and she agrees with me that you need to be punished."

For the second time that day Gemma burst into tears. "But please, Mr Davies, don't sack me, I won't moan about her again, I promise, so I do, I promise."

When she had calmed down George said, "Listen Gemma, this is not a work issue and you cannot be sacked for it. What it shows though is a lack of respect for your elders and betters. It shows a complete lack of respect for your Aunt who has kindly given up her house for you and who no doubt does your washing and puts a meal on the table. She has set rules and you refuse to obey them!" George thumped the desk.

Gemma started to cry once more. "I'm sorry," she sobbed.

"Now, your Aunt has given me permission to punish you in a way I think suitable, and I have decided to spank you."

Gemma held her hands tightly in front of her; the words seemed to have no effect. George almost felt like repeating them, but instead he said, "Gemma, come here please."

She walked around to his chair. George pushed it back away from the desk. Fortunately she was wearing a short summer dress; he took a deep breath and, as Gemma started to regain composure, he pulled her over his knee. She let out a cry but didn't struggle. George's Wandering Hand moved up to her skirt and pushed it up. She was wearing pink knickers which provided a nice cladding for her firm, eighteen-year-old buttocks. He raised his hand in the air and gave her a sharp smack. Then another. She cried out but the bank walls were thick and no one would hear. He waited to see if there was any reaction from her. There was none. She was actually very compliant and obsequious, and he knew she would take any punishment he chose to give. She definitely had a fear of authority. George gave her pretty knickers another spank and then pulled them down. Now he had her beautiful moon-like orbs at his mercy, white and virgin and exposed. He raised his right hand again. It came down with all the force he could muster. He started to spank her; right check, left check, he spanked and spanked and spanked. All the time he berated her for her disobedience towards her Aunt. And as he spanked he used different techniques, sometimes using an upward motion and cutting the buttocks from below, sometimes a full frontal assault. He did not relent until Gemma's backside was well and truly tanned. When he had finished he let her lie over his knee for a while. She was convulsed in sobs, but she did not move away. George let his fingers explore her virgin pussy, and as he expected she was moist. He let a finger probe her sex and push into her. He fingered her for a while, and watched her squirm and wriggle on his lap. Then he let her get up and gave her his white handkerchief so she could dry her eyes and blow her nose.

He stood up, and without saying a word, he roughly grabbed her by the scruff of the neck and threw her over the desk. Damn it! He was just too turned on and desperate for relief. He dropped his trousers and pushed her dress up again. Then he fucked her doggy style. He just had to hammer his swollen cock into her tight pussy as she groaned and gripped the edge of the desk.

"You want to go out and get fucked by all and sundry," he said, "well, I'll show you how it's done, young lady."

He leaned against the desk as his cock erupted inside her.

"Mr Davies, I'm not sure you should have done that," she murmured as he slumped back into his chair and she stood up and straightened her dress. "I don't think my Aunt would have thought of that as part of the punishment, so she wouldn't."

"She doesn't need to know, does she Gemma?" he said.

A few months later George stood looking out of the window watching the young mothers with their children and reflecting on the news he had just heard. Gemma was pregnant, and she wanted to keep the baby. He knew her Aunt had taken a belt to her when she found out, but to Gemma's credit she had not revealed the identity of the father. He knew he would have to phone Meredith, but first he wanted to speak to Gemma again. It was rather thrilling. Maybe Gemma was right after all; maybe he was a square who needed to get with it.

Either way he had made his decision, and when Gemma returned to his office he said, "I've got a property I own around the corner. I'm going to let you live there rent free and I'll support you financially with the baby. Obviously, I'll have to tell my wife that I have a mistress, but you will be well set up. I will visit and we will resume our affair."

"Thank you, Mr Davies," Gemma said. "Thank you so much."

When Gemma left the office he picked up the phone and called Meredith. She took the news as well as could be expected in the circumstances; after all, it wasn't the first time he had imparted such tidings.

WHIP HAND

The Jockey's Tale

"You stupid, bitch!" Eddy thundered. "You've just been banned for four days for over use of the whip!"

Tina placed her head in her hands and slunk down onto the bench. "I can't get used to these new BHA rules," she said. "They're so bloody stupid."

"Well, if you want to turn pro you'll have to get used to it!" Eddy's cold, hard voice echoed around the empty changing room. Next door Tina could hear the light-hearted banter of the male jockeys getting changed after the race - the same race she had been in. As usual Tina was the only female jockey riding and often changed on her own. OK, there was Katy Walsh and Nina Carberry, but she wasn't quite in their league... yet.

Eddy hadn't finished. "And another thing I'm displeased about is that I told you to ride Willy Wonga at the back. You knew he would get tired in a three miler... it was a case of go careful and see how much was left in the tank at the end. You may have been able to snatch a place, but oh no, you had to gallop off ahead."

Tina had enjoyed it. Leading the pack. Her horse out in front, the wind ripping through her thin silks as her horse galloped at thirty mph.

"Sir Duncan is furious with you, my girl. Willy Wonga is the best horse he has owned and he came last because you couldn't follow simple bloody instructions! You might lose your job and then you'd be for it."

Tears welled up in Tina's eyes; it wasn't easy being a conditional jockey, and she was desperate to succeed, to compete with the men. But she had done wrong; she knew that she should not have raced ahead... but she was leading at the last... she was in sight of the winning post... it had been a bad jump from the moment Willy Wonga had taken off; she had crashed through the top of the birch and been lucky to stay on him. One foot had come out of a stirrup as Willy Wonga wobbled and veered dangerously to the right. Maybe Eddy was right. Maybe she had pushed him too hard and he had put in a tired jump. For whatever reason she had messed up badly and nearly taken another horse out of the race. Fortunately, she had been able to steady him but by the time she regained control Willy Wonga had completely lost his stride and a number of horses passed her. In the event, Willy Wonga had been so winded he barely limped over the finish line... in last position. To compound her agony she had given him a few "reminders" with her whip that earned her a pointless ban. It was frustration on her part that had earned her a four day ban. Nothing more and nothing less and she knew she had acted badly.

Eddy had been quiet for a few seconds. Tina looked up; *don't let him see you're upset*, she told herself. She took in his handsome, rugged features; the dark eyes that glinted underneath the rim of his Trilby - the eyes that made her feel so uncomfortable whenever she found him staring at her when she was mucking out the stables or exercising a horse. She frequently blushed in his presence, but now it was Eddy who was red - red with rage.

He came closer and almost whispered, "In my father's day, my girl, you'd have taken a thrashing for disobedience like that."

Tina could feel his breath on her neck and it excited her. There was something magnetic about a powerful, authoritative man. She felt weak and puny and submissive. Eddy seized her by the arm and yanked her to her feet. He grabbed her riding crop off the peg.

"In fact, my girl, it's time you were taught a few lessons," Eddy hissed. "And not just about your failure to follow race orders. There are one or two other little gripes I have against you." Eddy roughly pushed her in front of him.

"You're hurting my arm, Eddy!" Tina objected. The grip was certainly vicelike. Her slender arm was like a twig in his large, forceful hand.

"It'll be more than your arm that gets hurt in a minute, my girl." He moved closer to her. His mouth was in kissing distance. She could smell the polo mint he'd been sucking. "You're going to get your arse whipped with the same whip that's led to that four day ban. And as I thrash your arse you can reflect on why you felt the need to beat a horse which had no chance of winning and why you failed to follow race orders. Is that clear?"

"Yes," Tina whispered. "I won't do it again. I don't need to be thrashed; I've learnt my lesson. Honest I have. I feel really bad about how I've behaved. Even before you came in I was sitting there reflecting on how stupid I've been."

"No one learns a lesson until they've felt real pain," Eddy said. "Words come cheap, Tina, and they teach nothing. Actions speak louder than words, my girl, and I'm going to show you how displeased I am by punishing you."

"No, please," Tina pleaded, on the verge of bursting into tears. But she knew the plea was in vain, that Eddy had already decided on her chastisement and there would be no changing his mind - just like that time when she had arrived late for work after oversleeping and been walloped in the stable.

"Do you want to keep your job, or don't ya?" Eddy questioned.

"Yes, of course..."

"Then take a thrashing."

"But it's the twenty-first century - you can't treat people like this, Eddy, you just can't, it's wrong."

"Oh, can't I?" Eddy snorted. "You've been banned for four days for overuse of the whip, so I'm going to show you what that feels like. I'm going to give you a few reminders in the same way you gave poor old Willy Wonga a few reminders."

Tina found herself being dragged forward. She was still wearing her racing skills and jodhpurs, her black boots and clothes splattered with mud. Eddy moved his hand from her arm and grabbed her collar, then walked her across the change room, the toes of her boots barely touching the floor, and then he flung her onto a large table. The padding that encased her breasts and chest cushioned her as she sprawled on the hard wooden surface.

There was silence. Stillness. She sensed that Eddy was disrobing. Removing his hat. His jacket. His scarf. Rolling up his sleeves. Tina lay on the table, too scared to move. Frightened. If she tried to fight the draconian punishment, what would happen? No more races for a start; more mucking out, more cleaning duties and no race riding. And if she left no one else would employ her. She knew she wasn't the best rider there was and life would be hard outside of Eddy's yard. No, she had to lay there and think of Ireland.

Suddenly the whip was sailing through the air. It cut into her buttocks, jerking tears from her eyes. The pain wracked her body, sent a tingling sensation up her spine - she had never felt anything like it before. When Eddy walloped her in the stable it had been with leather reins which had not hurt too much, but this was serious, this was painful. A second stroke bit into the thin white of her jodhpurs. Tina winced and gripped the table's edge. She tried to repress a scream of agony. A third stroke laced her backside. Then another cracking stroke rained down. The next lash of the whip brought forth an involuntary cry that she could no longer repress, as did the fifth and sixth. Her body lurched forward, she could resist the pain no longer.

"Please Eddy, stop! *Stop!*"

Eddy took no notice. He was building up a head of steam; first the right buttock and then the left. Whack! Crack! Wallop! Tina recoiled as each stroke thumped home on her defenceless buttocks. She cried, she wept, she pleaded but Eddy was in no mood for relenting. She had been banned for overuse of the whip and now she was finding out what it really felt like. Not that Eddy was doing it because of the horse's welfare. No, to him it was more the fact that Tina had failed to follow instructions and got herself unnecessarily banned because she was annoyed with herself and the stupid mistake she had made at the last. There were other reasons too, of course... Tina knew that... unspoken reasons.

The whip came down again and slashed across her buttocks. Tina had never experienced pain like it. The jodhpurs offered no real protection.

"Stop Eddy, stop!" she sobbed, but she knew her words were in vain. Eddy had a hold of her, had her in his power and she was being thrashed like an errant child in a Nineteenth century novel. The whip rained terror on her buttocks, slicing and dicing her. Her backside became so numb she almost lost all feeling in her buttocks.

Finally she heard the whip drop to the floor. She lay on the table panting, crying, whining. Then she felt Eddy behind her. Her buttocks were warm and painful and bruised. He forced her jodhpurs down. Pushed them down so they tore as they gathered around her ankles. Tina, knew what was coming next. She had caught Eddy in bed with a scatty brunette secretary and in the stable with two stable girls, Sandra and Patsy, and she guessed that part of his rage with her was due to her uncompromising insistence that she was not another notch on his bedpost. He had often come on to her and now, after the flogging, she did not have the energy to resist the inevitable. But was it just a lack of energy? Something inside her tingled with anticipation. The thrashing had made her wet and aroused. She knew she too was going to experience Eddy's much travelled cock, and this time she was not going to resist, though she hated herself for giving in to him. She grabbed the edge of the table.

Behind her she could hear Eddy unzipping his trousers. This is the price I must pay, she thought to herself. She didn't want to lose the job as conditional jockey and the Grade 3 race at Caldwell Park racecourse had been her biggest yet, and that was why she'd been so frustrated when she made such an elementary mistake - she had been sure she was going to win. Then Eddy would have had to give her more races.

She waited for his cock to enter her and was surprised when nothing happened. Instead, he came to the side of the table and the next thing Tina felt was the hard splat as his bare hand impacted on her raw buttocks.

"I think you need a few more, my girl," he said, as he continued to smack her on the right buttock and then her left and then her right again. Right, left, right, left. Sharp, rapid smacks. Tina winced. There was no doubt that Eddy had a huge amount of spanking experience and was well practiced in the art. As Tina lay over the table trying to cope with the pain she wistfully wondered how many girls he had actually spanked - and fucked, for that matter.

After the thrashing with the whip her backside was as sensitive as sunburnt skin. She closed her eyes but still the tears seeped out. She had a high pain threshold - you had to have to be a jump jockey - but even so she had never felt as sore.

Eddy spanked her five or six more times and then he stopped. Tina remained slumped over the table. Defeated. Deflated. Demoralised.

This time she could feel Eddy's large erection touching her thigh. He teased her with it by sliding the head over her buttocks.

"You've played your stupid chasing games with me for too long, Tina, my girl," he said. "I've seen you in the stables with Charlie and the others, but when I come a-knocking for a little bit of TLC you reject me. Now why is that, Tina?"

"I don't know, Eddy," she said. "I'm sorry."

"Well, you're going to take a good shafting now and you'll enjoy it, is that clear?"

Tina admitted it was. She folded her arms around her head and lay still. She felt Eddy removing her jodhpurs and boots completely so she was bare from the waist down. Then she felt his cock, his big, hard cock squeezing between her legs. He was handsome but he was arrogant, and he was twenty years her senior, but she knew sooner or later he would bed her - all the stable boys and girls said as much.

"Never a pretty one escapes Eddy's grasp," one of the Irish jockeys had told her once. So that was that, Eddy would fuck her. End of. And over the jockeys table at Caldwell Park racetrack seemed as good a place as any; at least no prying eyes would see, though she knew Eddy would drop a word into one of the jockey's ears that he'd had Tina. It was how he operated. He never boasted directly about whom he had fucked, but just let rumours spread like wildfire through the stables. He liked to see his conquests blush when questioned by other riders about their liaisons with him. He liked to see them squirm. And she had to admit that the thrashing and the spanking had made her rather horny; especially now the pain was infused with a lovely warm glow.

Eddy pushed his erect cock into her moist slit. Tina yelped as she felt it start to make its journey into her. She didn't really want sex, not with Eddy, but she knew she had little choice; if she wanted to remain working at his stables then she would have to succumb. Inch by inch Eddy pressed his cock into her. Then he was behind her with his hands on her red-hot buttocks fucking her for all she was worth. He pressed his cock further and further into her, then withdrew and pushed forward again. Tina

23

jerked on the table, her breasts and padding offering little in the way of protection. She almost giggled at the thought of Eddy behind her, panting and rutting and grinding while she lay inert over the table, putting in no effort at all.

"I've wanted to fuck you for ages, Tina, you artful little minx,' he grunted. 'It's a pity it's taken a thrashing for you to see sense."

"Sorry," Tina said. Perhaps she had been foolish to resist for so long. Maybe if she had been more compliant earlier she would have got more rides... and not just with Eddy.

A few moments later he sank his cock into her with immense force, and exploded inside her.

Tina sighed and closed her eyes and felt her inner sanctum shudder with an enormous orgasm. She had to admit Eddy certainly knew how to fuck. So she was to be another notch on his bedpost after all. Still, at least she was now able to compare notes with the other girls in the stable.

When he had finished Eddy pulled up his trousers and straightened his clothing. At the door he stopped. Looked back. Smiled.

"Don't worry, Tina," he said. "We all make mistakes... and that four day ban may not be such a bad thing."

Tina still lay on the table - her head in her arms. She turned to him.

"How do you mean?"

"Well, once you've mucked out, if I've not got any races to go to you can come over to the cottage for breakfast and we can see where the day takes us."

Going to the cottage for breakfast meant you were part of Eddy's inner sanctum and likely to get the best rides - though one of the rides was inevitably Eddy.

"Thank you," she said. "I'd like that."

"Oh, and by the way, I keep Mr Stinger at the cottage to educate miscreant stable lasses and riders."

Tina had heard all about "Mr Stinger", the cane he kept at his cottage. As well as the cane he also had a slipper, and a paddle. Just the other week Sandra had come back to the yard rubbing her tight jeans and crying. Apparently Eddy had slippered her because she'd taken too long for lunch for the second time that week. Tina had to admit that she rather admired Eddy for walloping Sandra, who she did not like, and told Sandra that, "At least you know where you stand with a disciplinarian like Eddy."

Sandra had not taken particularly kindly to the comment, and now Tina could understand why.

When Eddy had gone Tina lay contemplating the fate that had befallen her. Her first race in a Grade 3, a thrashing, and Eddy fucking her - all in one day. Caldwell Park Racecourse would certainly live long in her memory. She felt sorry for herself. Her buttocks were red and raw, and her fanny was sore and ached. The burning sensation in her backside fanned through her thighs and up her back. Her clitoris pulsed and her pussy still itched for relief; the thrashing had awakened her sexually just as it had done in the stable when he walloped her for being late. Through the agony was the ecstasy - a feeling of pleasure mingled, like twine, with the pain she was suffering.

It was some minutes before she moved. Slowly, she got completely undressed and stood naked before a tall mirror. She admired the neat branding the whip had made on her shapely bottom; the raw lines that Eddy had cut into her flesh; the palm-prints from his large hands. She had been thrashed and fucked and she felt all the better for it.

She went to the shower and turned it on; the warm water refreshed and invigorated and stung. She shampooed her long blonde hair and poured body lotion over her pert breasts. She let the water wash over her as she inserted a slender finger into her slit and let it roam freely. The anger of Eddy's voice came back to her, the authority, the control. She could still feel his firm grip on her arm, see the marks he'd left there. She closed her eyes and relived the journey to the table, the whip - her whip - menacing and awesome in all its terrible power. Her body shivered with involuntarily spasms and she moaned as she thought about the unbelievable event that had just befallen her. She, Tina Edwards, a farmer's daughter from County Donegal had been thrashed, just like the nuns had walloped her in convent school and her dad had spanked her when she was little... and just like Eddy had beaten her in the stable.

The warm water caressed her injured buttocks and sent a tingling sensation through her nervous system as she frigged herself with greater urgency.

The hand on her back made her jump.

"Hi Tina, we just came to see you were all right, so we did." It was Barry, a young Irish jockey Tina had heard laughing in the changing room next door. A flop of ginger hair hung over his cheeky eyes, and beside him was the scrawny figure of Sean, another conditional jockey. Tina folded her arms to cover her breasts, then quickly covered her vagina. The two lads laughed.

"Never you mind that, Tina Edwards, we've seen it all before - least ways, I have. We've been watching you for ages, so we have," Barry said.

The two jockeys stood before her with identikit racecourse white towels wrapped around their waists. Clearly, her presence was having an effect on them!

"Anyways, if it makes you feel better you can have a look at Sean's riding tackle."

With that remark Barry pulled away Sean's towel. Sean laughed and jumped back, desperately trying to cover his erect cock. Tina smiled.

"And mine as well, while we're at it." Barry too let his towel drop, revealing a fat, red-tipped monster, which appeared incongruous in relation to his diminutive frame. Barry made no move to conceal his penis - in fact, he seemed rather proud of it.

Both jockeys stood before her, naked. Small of stature and gaunt and thin with constant dieting, their bony frames seemed almost boyish, yet the erect penises told her they were young men in need of a moist cunt to penetrate. Tina's plight was all too obvious to her. She smiled submissively, knowing she was about to be fucked - by both of them.

Barry took one pace forward into the spray of water that fell onto Tina. His fingers made a grab for her pussy, an index finger inserted itself between her moist lips and tickled her innermost sex. Tina released an involuntary moan.

"Now, where did you get up to with frigging yourself after Mr Chapman whipped you?"

"You heard?"

"Of course we heard. You couldn't very well not hear the noise you twos were making in here. Poor Sean and I were just trying to catch a bit of kip on the bench so we were."

Tina released a gasp as Barry's finger probed further into her slippery interior; feeling out her g-spot, sending her into raptures of pleasure.

"Mr Chapman is a fine one with the whip, so he is," Barry said. "Perhaps you'd

25

better be a good girl in future and just follow race orders and not go and get getting ahead of yourself and collecting a ban for over-whipping. Mr Chapman wants to make a name for his self now he's taken over from his father and he doesn't want a young upstart like you to spoil it. Now, that wouldn't do, would it?"

Barry pressed his mouth against hers. They fell back to the wall of the shower fumbling each others' bodies.

Suddenly Tina felt a hard object being thrust into her. Billy was fucking her up against the shower wall. Slowly, rhythmically his throbbing member slid back and forth like a well-oiled piston. Tina's scolded buttocks slipped up and down the wet tiles in time to his metronomic movements. Her buttocks splayed out on the cool white ceramics, finding relief from the simmering heat. Over Barry's shoulder Tina could see Sean drinking in the scene. As Barry rammed her harder and deeper, Sean adopted the riding position, legs akimbo. He grabbed hold of his cock and masturbated. Tina watched wide-eyed and incredulous as Sean's penis first dripped and then sprayed forth a creamy white mix, which intermingled with the shower water and swirled down into the drain. She felt her vagina tighten around the thicker member that had invaded her. Her muscles clenched and squeezed the alien pole.

"Oh, God!" she shrieked.

Suddenly Barry's spunk burst forth inside her. She slumped as she came too; Barry's cock pinned her to the wall and kept her from slipping down the slippery tiles.

"That was good, Barry," Tina panted, "so fucking good."

"Now, it's time to get you dry," Barry said. He took her by the hand and led her to the sauna, Sean following behind like an obedient cocker spaniel.

Barry pushed open the sauna door. Tina collapsed onto a wooden bench, already the steam helping her pores cleanse. Sean sat beside her.

"It's over to you, mate," Barry said, then left them, closing the door behind him.

Tina felt Sean's hand on her thigh. She looked at his features, drawn with dieting, his freckled face beaming contently. Tina guessed he was still a virgin. She moved his hand up her leg until it found her cunt. Guided by her, Sean started to finger her. As the heat opened further her perspiring pores, Sean's fingers tentatively probed her sex. After a while Tina rolled him onto his back and rode him, like she had ridden Willy Wonga, back and forth, back and forth, slowly, rhythmically she rode the virgin jockey as his cock rose up inside her cunt. The smile never left his freckled face. Tina rode on, moving up and down on her mount until he squirted his spunk into her, and Tina clenched the pulsing penis as she too climaxed.

Both staggered from the sauna and kissed. Barry was waiting for them.

"Have you done the business, Sean?" he asked.

Sean nodded excitedly.

"I told you Tina would see you right, so I did."

The lads grabbed their towels and left the changing room. Tina made her way back to her peg and pulled her panties on, wincing a little as the cool material cosseted her bum, then on with her jeans and top. She then dried her hair and zipped up her padded coat. She packed her things away in her bag and was ready to go, glancing at her mobile phone. Three missed calls and a voice message. Tina stuffed it into her pocket, anxious to leave. It was getting dark outside and the racecourse was empty. She guessed her car would be the last in the car park, that Barry and Sean would have gone, and she wanted to get home to a warm bed and a cup of cocoa. Once in the safe comfort of her car she played the voice message - it was from Eddy.

"*Meet me back at the cottage; I haven't finished with you yet, my girl. Oh no, Captain Ramrod wants some more Pussy and I want to introduce you to Mr Stinger. I trust your bum's still smouldering because when you get here, my girl, I'm going to reignite it. I have two good reasons to believe you may have been a very naughty girl again in the changing room... and the sauna. Let's hope you're not to saddle-sore tomorrow, because Mr Stinger's going to see some action before the night's out. Take my word for it, my girl, Mr Stinger's on the warpath.*"

Tina slunk down into her car seat and closed her eyes. She felt like crying. Her bum was burning still - all she wanted was a quiet night. She sighed and shook her head. Then with a quiet determination she started the engine; it had been a long day, and clearly it was not over yet - far from it.

SLIPPERING SUSAN

The Brother's Tale

I sit in my car watching a magpie pressing its beak under the bark of a tree as it searches for grubs. Its beak investigates and sometimes finds food and sometimes it doesn't. In a manner of speaking, that's what I do now. I work as a psychiatrist and I get under peoples' skin; explore why my patients are the way they are. My interest in the human mind started with a curiosity about sado-masochism and an interest in spanking which goes back to an event or events which took place in my teens. Not many people would have as clear a recollection as I have as to why I have this strange fetish: to spank, to cane, to wallop, to smack, to belt... but Susan has, oh yes; Susan has...

The date was Saturday, 7th December, 1985. Period. As the Americans say. That was the day I caught the spanking bug. Maybe there was some seed there to start with, some tiny speck of mind matter that was a fertile place for my interest to take hold. Maybe. Certainly, I grew up in a home where the threat of spanking or a smack was fairly commonplace, both at school and at home. My dad was an advocate, my mother was not. We lived in a suburban detached house - a Swiss chalet style with the kitchen at the front. Both mum and dad worked and we were a pretty normal family. At the time of the incident I was sixteen and my sister, Susan, was eighteen.

She was tall (taller than dad at any rate), slim and blonde. I suppose she was attractive but you don't look at your sister like that, do you? She had just started work as a secretary and, after two failures had just passed her driving test in dad's car. He had been her instructor on the third occasion.

Susan was like any other teenager and liked to go out; she had boyfriends and girlfriends and generally liked to go out late and come back in the early hours - if at all - and this caused friction between her and dad, who was a bit conservative and very much of the "you don't do that under my roof" school. Mum was the peacemaker, softening and intervening as Susan, who took after dad and was quite fiery, crossed swords with him. So, at the time of the incident, things had been brewing between Susan and dad for some time. It was the usual teenage clashes.

"What time do you call this?"

"You'll have to leave home if you can't get home at a proper hour."

There was never any threat of a slap of spanking. Those days were long gone, and anyway my mother would not have allowed it. Instead it was verbal jousting with Susan giving as good as she got and antagonising dad.

When she passed her test dad honestly believed things would improve and that Susan would get home earlier. He helped her pass her test and he really thought once she had share of the family car she would mend her ways. The family car. Dad's pride and joy. At first he had been reluctant to place Susan on the insurance, but assurances about her keeping better hours and the safety factor made him relent.

So to the Saturday night. Susan was going clubbing with two friends and wanted to drive. She begged dad, who relented, under pressure from mum who emotionally blackmailed him with tales of women alone. When she came downstairs all done up and ready to go out for an evening, wearing a tight black pencil skirt, high stiletto heels, a silky blouse and her black leather jacket, dad saw the heels and insisted she change to drive. In fact, so concerned had he been about her driving in heels he had bought her a pair of plimsolls.

"Make sure you wear those plimsolls I bought you," he said. "They're in the cupboard under the stairs."

"Yes dad," Susan replied, but I could tell she had as much chance of changing her fashionable stilettos as an Eskimo has of getting a suntan. Dad walked back to the sitting room to watch TV, Susan collected the car keys from the kitchen, moved her purse from her work bag to her clutch bag and left the house, four inches taller than she should have been. Soon she was roaring off down the road.

Susan had worn heels on many occasions when driving - little did dad know - so neither mum nor I thought anything of it.

It was gone three a.m. when I was woken - we were all woken - by a sound downstairs. Mum was the first up and found Susan blubbing in the kitchen like a two year old. At first we thought she had been attacked and something terrible had happened to her, but gradually a different story emerged. She had not been attacked - but dad's precious car had been.

Susan had gone to pick up two friends and they went clubbing. On the way home Susan dropped them off. The last one lived in a cul-de-sac and Susan had to drive to the end of it, but due to parked cars was unable to turn around. Instead of reversing back up the narrow street (reversing wasn't Susan's strong point) she tried to turn around and hit not one but two parked cars, damaging the front and back of ours. Susan sobbed the story out to mum as they hugged in the kitchen, but dad overheard it all. He stood with his hands in the pockets of his dressing gown listening to the tale and becoming increasingly angry. Eventually he went to the cupboard under the stairs and took out a flashlight and marched to the front door.

I followed him outside. He turned the flashlight on and inspected the damage to the front and back of the car. I could tell he was fuming as he literally did not say a word - always a sure sign that he was just one word, one step, one murmur away from a volcanic eruption. Fortunately dad did not explode often, but when he did you sure didn't want to be around!

He flashed the light through the car windows. I was not too sure why at the time but all was to come blatantly clear when he returned to the kitchen where Susan was still being hugged by mum, and reassured that everything would be all right.

She was wrong. Dad was angry. Very angry.

"You didn't wear the plimsolls I bought you, did you?" he bellowed.

Susan looked stunned. She had expected anything but this. She had probably forgotten all about them.

"They wouldn't have helped!" she cried. "It was the stupid, stupid street, it was too narrow and there was nowhere to turn around and too many parked cars and..."

Mum stood away from her. "Susan, your father told you not to wear high heels when you're driving, now, why didn't you wear the plimsolls he bought you?"

"What, and have all my friends laugh at me?"

"You can't drive in heels," mum said calmly. "You should have worn flat shoes; if not plimsolls then some others." In truth mum was being a bit disingenuous because she, like me, had seen Susan leave wearing high heels and said nothing.

"What do you know? You refuse to get in the car with me. You don't know what I drive like."

"But you damaged your father's car tonight through careless driving!"

"I'm not a careless driver!"

"Sorry, Susan, but you are. Your father told you to wear plimsolls and you went out in stilettos because you wanted to impress your friends."

"I did not want to impress my fucking friends! I don't give a fuck what they think. Or what you think! You can't drive. Oh, too scared, aren't you! So why have a go at me, you cow?"

"I'll not be spoken to like that, Susan, now take that back!" mum shrieked.

"Cow. Bitch. Slag."

Dad had been quietly observing the fireworks between mother and daughter - now he intervened. He took Susan by the arm and squeezed her leather jacket tightly.

"You've gone too far, young lady," he said through firmly gritted teeth.

Mum started to cry. "I'm not standing here being insulted. You can do what you want with her, George, I disown her." With which she left the room.

Susan probably didn't realise the damage she had done in upsetting her ally - especially one who opposed corporal punishment. Now I realise that she had picked on mum because she realised she was a soft target compared to dad, and wanted to vent her anger about the damage to the car on someone. And in fairness to Susan, who knew if the shoes really were to blame for the accident?

Dad had become remarkably calm. Unnaturally so.

Then he uttered the words that made my cock stand on edge, the words which released an involuntary shiver, the words that sounded so nice I've recited them a thousand times to myself. Words with a thousand meanings, but only one meaning to me.

"Fetch the plimsolls, John; they're in the cupboard under the stairs."

Over the years I have replayed and replayed those words in my mind.

"Fetch the plimsolls, John; they're in the cupboard under the stairs."

I loved the sound of them. The cool, matter-of-fact way my dad delivered them. As I say they meant everything to me... and nothing. Was he thinking what I was thinking? I was slightly thrown by the plural - surely he only needed one? Maybe I was wrong.

Maybe.

The look in his eye and the firm grip with which he held Susan's arm told me I was right. She breathed uneasily. Her mascara had run and she dabbed a tissue to her eyes. She didn't know. She had no idea. Not like me. Not like dad. We knew. I could see it in his eyes. I knew that look. It was the look after the rage. The look of a man who knew exactly what he was doing. The look of a man determined to get his own way.

I scurried up the hall and, with shaking hands, undid the lock on the door, I turned on the light and picked up two new, unworn plimsolls. I pulled them to my chest as if they were precious pets and, with my other hand, pushed my cock down inside my pyjamas - God, I hoped no one would noticed my erection. Please God, make dad do it, I prayed. Please God, make dad spank her.

I returned to the kitchen and held out the plimsolls. Dad made no move to take them - in fact, he ignored them. Instead, he started to move. Susan was dragged in his wake as he moved, not quickly but slowly. He walked out of the kitchen and along the hall. He pushed open the door of the dining room. Susan was beside him and then behind him. I followed; holding my valuable cargo. The curtains weren't drawn and I could see the orange glow of streetlights. Moonlight glittered on our small fishpond. The alabaster heron that stood to one side of the pond looked ghostly and ethereal. All was calm, all was peaceful.

"Light," dad said.

I turned it on. I felt like I was helping a surgeon in a hospital. Handing scalpels and scissors and other surgical instruments. This was an operation and no mistake - a very long overdue operation.

He took a dining chair in one hand and turned it around so it faced the door - faced me. Did Susan understand? Had the full enormity of what was about to happen sunk in? Had she realised that for the first time in her life something dad had previously threatened her with was now going to happen. That mum, the person who intervened, the person who always stopped corporal punishment before dad had an opportunity to apply it, was gone, taken out of the equation by dint of Susan's own rudeness. Now dad had an opportunity; an opportunity he'd perhaps awaited for some years.

To this day I don't know if Susan realised what was going to happen. She certainly didn't make a fuss until it was too late, so I suspect she didn't. I think she was in a state of shock. She says she can't remember that much about the incident. I do. I remember it like it was yesterday.

Dad sat down and in the same movement pulled my sister over his knee. Her black pencil skirt stretched tightly over her firm buttocks, her blonde hair tumbled to the carpet, covering her face. She let out a yelp. She struggled. But dad held her tightly. Her right hand spread protectively across her buttocks. Now she knew.

"You can't!" she complained. "I'm eighteen. I'm at work, for God's sake."

Dad didn't bother to answer - this was not the time for niceties. Without being asked I offered the plimsolls again. This time dad took one. Holding the other plimsoll I felt like a ball boy at Wimbledon waiting to throw a tennis ball to a player. I prayed dad would not send me out of the room. He didn't.

"When you passed your test you promised me faithfully you were going to wear plimsolls and not stilettos when you drove, didn't you?" he admonished.

"Yes," Susan sobbed, her voice muffled by her hair. "Yes, but it wasn't the shoes, it was the stupid, stupid road that caused the accident. I'm never going to Lorraine's again."

Dad ignored her. "I bought you a pair of plimsolls, but have you worn them?"

"No," Susan whimpered.

"Well, tonight they are going to be put to good use," dad said. He held her tightly. Susan wriggled and attempted in vain to protect her buttocks with her hand, but dad brought the plimsoll down on her cotton-covered backside. The rubber sole made an almighty *thwack* as it impacted on Susan's bottom.

"Ouch!" she shrieked. "No, dad, no!"

He ignored her. He whacked her for a second time, but this time he caught Susan's fingers as she tried to stop the punishment.

"Put your hand down!" he yelled. "If you raise it once more I will wallop you so hard you won't sit down for a week!"

Her hand fell to the floor. She burst into tears. She surrendered.

Dad belaboured her that night. He really whacked her. He moved her up on his knee and went to work; multiple hard, hard, repetitive whacks like a machine gun. Susan cried and whined and wriggled but dad was determined. I had never before seen his face so red with anger. I would have loved it if the skirt had been taken down and she had been spanked on her bare bottom so I could have witnessed her checks taking on a rosy hue, but that would have been too much to ask. As it was I was witness to a good five minutes - and five minutes is a long time when you're over someone's knee and that someone's spanking the living daylights out of you. I was hot and bothered and frustrated, and at one point my cock seeped juices onto my leg. I just trembled and shivered as I witnessed the most erotic scene I have ever observed in my life, and because it was the first it was all the more powerful for it.

He spanked her countless times with that plimsoll that night. Susan cried and whined and yelled but he would not stop. The plimsoll crashed onto her buttocks time and time again. It was mum who stopped it. In the end she came downstairs and told him to stop, and Susan ran up to bed crying and rubbing her backside.

But that wasn't the end of the story - far from it. Bob was a friend of the family who lived around the corner and worked in a garage. He managed to get the car repaired at a good price and everyone was really thankful that the incident was over. Susan decided she didn't want to drive any more and, out of angst I guess, said she would take a taxi everywhere, and who could blame her?

Bob knew, of course, that Susan had damaged the car; dad had made it quite clear it wasn't him. So on Christmas Day, when he came round for dinner, as he usually did, it was inevitable that the full story would be revealed. Bob, I should say at this stage, was a widower as his wife had died young and he no children. He was slightly younger than dad but of a similar generation. He was good at DIY and would often help out with odd jobs for us, and in return receive a Sunday dinner, and as we had all known him for such a long time, in many ways he seemed like an "uncle" to us.

So that Christmas Day evening, with Susan sitting on the arm of mum's chair, wearing black trousers and a smart blouse, dad told Bob how he had slippered her with a plimsoll as she had caused the accident by wearing high heels. Bob smiled broadly, and I knew that smile; it must have been similar to the one I'd had on my face when dad gave the order to get the plimsolls. Susan blushed to the roots of her blond hair but Bob could not keep his eyes off her. And when dad had finished the tale of woe Bob said, "So you had a sore backside that night, Susan then, didn't you?"

Her foot kicked against the armchair, and mum rubbed her back gently. She was so embarrassed she could not speak, but Bob was not going to let the matter drop.

"You should have done what your dad told you to do," he said.

Susan muttered an almost inaudible, "I know."

"Don't go on about it, George," mum said to dad. "You know she's embarrassed."

She certainly was, and Bob and I were enjoying her embarrassment immensely.

"I don't want to go on about it," dad said. "But I can tell Bob; he's a family friend."

Mum was exasperated. "Yes, but don't go on about it - its Christmas Day. Let's talk about happy things."

Little did mum know that to me, Bob and possibly even dad the topic was a very pleasant one. Seeing Susan blush and extremely embarrassed was delightful and worth a couple of presents. So before the subject was wound up completely I added fuel to the fire.

"You deserved it though, didn't you Susan, the way you spoke to mum an' all."

Dad had skimmed over that part about Susan's verbal onslaught on mum, and I thought it would help to add to the picture of a truculent teenager who had received a much overdue spanking.

"Why? What did she say to you, June?" Bob asked.

Mum paused, then said, "She was rude."

"Very rude," I said. "And the irony is mum hates corporal punishment."

So started a debate on the merits of corporal punishment, with Bob and dad advocating the "short, sharp shock" as a cure all for the ills of society. I didn't say much, but when I did I turned to Susan and asked, "What do you think, sis?"

"I dunno."

"You deserved the spanking dad gave you though, didn't you?"

"I suppose so," she acknowledged.

I looked over at dad; a wide grin on his face. Susan had deserved it. We all knew that. Even she admitted it.

That New Year's Eve Bob was having a small party at his house. Susan dressed up in a black leather miniskirt and a silky camisole top - with her obligatory four inch black patent stilettos. We all traipsed around to Bob's house, just around the corner, carrying some wine and soft drinks.

The party was a fairly dull affair with only us and a few neighbours. Susan helped Bob put out the chicken wings and dips and offered around plates of picky bits and was generally in good humour, despite not being out with her friends. She had forgone the opportunity to go clubbing with her friends, which was very un-Susan-like, but I quickly realised why, for on arrival Bob had said how nice Susan looked, and during the evening I noticed that on more than one occasion his hand drifted to Susan's leather-clad buttocks and gave them a little squeeze. I even noticed her buttock twitch in anticipation of Bob's hand whenever he was near to her. I don't think anyone else noticed as it mainly occurred in the kitchen, and all the other guests were in the living room. I may have been a bit naive and yet to lose my virginity, but I certainly knew flirting when I saw it.

At first I was a bit surprised. As I say, we had known Bob for years and he was some twenty-five years Susan's senior, but there was no doubt about the fact that she blushed around him and giggled at his jokes. She didn't have a boyfriend; perhaps she liked the older man?

I decided to help Susan and Bob and started to collect dishes and drinks from the kitchen, and at one point I confronted him.

"You like my sister's bum, don't you?"

He smiled. "Look, John, your sister's attractive, there's nothing wrong in us having some fun, is there?"

"Dad wouldn't like it."

"He doesn't need to know, does he?"

"I guess not."

"Anyway, what would he do if he thought we were flirting?" Bob asked.

I couldn't resist it. "Spank her, I hope."

Bob laughed heartily. "You've got a downer on your sister, eh? What's she ever done to hurt you?"

I blushed. "Nothing."

Instantly Bob knew my secret. "Ah, you witnessed Susan being spanked, didn't you?"

"Yes," I mumbled, and left the room just as Susan arrived.

After the midnight chimes the party started to wind down and the guests drifted off home. Susan volunteered to stay behind to help Bob clear up, and I spied an opportunity to stay as well, saying I'd help too and walk Susan home. I think Bob and Susan were a little disappointed as they'd obviously seen an opportunity for some further flirting... if not other things.

Even so, Susan and I went to work clearing up the glasses and the plates. It wasn't long before Bob came into the living room and drew up a chair and sat down.

"Come here, Susan," he said.

She sashayed over to him.

"That skirt and heels make you look like a prostitute," he began. "And I'm going to punish you for it."

"No, please, don't," she said in a wistful, sexy voice.

"I'm afraid I have to," he said. "Your dad's done it, now it's my turn. I told you on Christmas Day that if you came to my house looking like a tart and wearing high heels you would get spanked, and you've done it on purpose to provoke me."

So that was it! Following dad's revelation about spanking Susan, Bob had obviously made some joke to her when they were alone that if she dressed like a tart on New Year's she would get spanked! And Susan had duly obliged! I had thought the leather mini was a bit much for the small gathering, but it all fell into place. Susan wanted to be spanked!

"Please, no, I didn't mean too!" she begged. She played the part of the errant teenager to perfection. The banter continued for a few minutes. Finally Susan was pulled over Bob's knee. He raised his hand high into the air. My cock was in overdrive.

"I'm not being spanked with my brother here!" she protested.

"Go outside," Bob ordered with a wink.

I left the room, but was still looking through the slightly open door, although Susan could not see me.

Bob brought his hand down on her buttocks once, twice, three times - smack, spank, smack. Susan whined and wriggled, but unlike the thrashing she had taken from dad she was enjoying it and her protests were false. When Bob finished his initial spanks he undid the popper on her skirt and eased down the zip. The skirt was pushed to her ankles. Then for the lacy red knickers - down in one swipe. Once Susan's arse was clear of cladding the real spanking began, and for the first time I got to see a genuine spanked backside. Bob lifted his hand again and again - smack, wallop, spank. He worked away on her butt like a true professional, though I didn't realise it then - right cheek, left check, right check. It would be another four years before I found out that Bob was an authentic spanker who enjoyed the single life and often spanked females in his home. Susan's story must have been manna from heaven. At the time all I could do was watch in amazement as Bob's deft hand beat out a rat-a-tat rhythm on Susan's backside, turning it red and crimson and leaving large handprints on her buttocks.

Bob worked himself into a lather spanking Susan, but this was not the punishment she had received at the hands of dad. No, this was a pleasure spanking and Susan did not struggle; she placed her legs out straight and scissor-kicked with each strike, her high heels clunking together.

On and on it went until he finally finished and pushed her to the floor. Then, unbelievably, with Susan lying on the carpet, he released his massive cock. He held it over her, and then he straddled and laid on top of her, and as I stared he eased his erection into her damp slit. Susan cried out in ecstasy as he rocked back and forth, back and forth. He fucked her well and truly that night, as I stood and watched at the door. Finally he shuddered and heaved and panted.

"Fuck me, Susan," he panted, "that was good! You wouldn't believe how long I've wanted to fuck you."

She ran a painted nail down his check. "Thanks Bob," she said. "You're wonderful. Where's John?"

Quickly I retreated to the kitchen.

"John, have you been watching?" Susan called. "Have you?"

I started to clatter around, then I reappeared at the door, red-faced and embarrassed.

"I... I've been clearing up," I stumbled.

"No, you haven't, you've been watching."

Bob was standing. He'd done his trousers up. "Don't worry, Susan, he won't say anything and if he does he'll have me to deal with."

I shivered. I felt scared. I had never seen that threatening side of Bob before.

'I won't say anything, honest," I promised.

"Better not, see," he said, and raised his fist in my direction.

By this time Susan had her skirt on and was fluffing out her hair.

"You two get off home," Bob said. "I'll clear the rest away."

Susan and I walked in silence. I could not quite believe what I had just witnessed.

"Please don't tell mum or dad about tonight," she said as we reached our front door.

"Of course not," I said. And I didn't. God knows if Susan became one of Bob's regulars. I don't think she did, and I don't think she was like me; left with a lifetime's obsession with S&M - which led me to become a psychiatrist.

That night, despite the late hour, I pulled the snake for all it was worth. I had never seen anything so erotic in my life. Like the magpie pushing its beak under the bark, you never know what you might discover when you forage, and that's why I love my job.

TEACHING TOM
The Manageress's Tale

Tom Prendley blushed to the roots of his blond hair. His hand shook as he picked up a cup of coffee.

"Bet you are!"

"Don't torment him, Sandra," Tom's manageress, Janice, chided.

Sandra, seated at the canteen table, rocked back and forth, her gaze never left the silent Tom. Did Sandra secretly fancy her newest recruit? Janice wondered; she turned on her black her high heels and walked to the self-service food counter, where she grabbed a cup of tea and a cake.

"Janice, can I have a word?"

The suited form of Malcolm approached, holding a file. She couldn't even get a rest during her tea break. It was going to be a long day.

As Malcolm talked about "best lines" and "profits" Janice found her gaze falling on the shy nineteen-year-old at the other table who had been transferred to her from Electricals. Sandra was now talking to her colleagues, Tracey and Zoe - who were dubbed The Three Musketeers because they were always together. Janice reflected that her two sons had been far more worldly-wise than Tom when they had been nineteen. Now they were both married and had children of their own, and after a lifetime of womanising, their father had left the family home to be with the best friend of her oldest son's wife, which meant Janice was now living on her own.

Still, she enjoyed her job and had made the Fashion Department one of the best, despite Tom, for whom she had a soft spot, beginning to let her down by making constant mistakes. It was just a pity he was so naïve, which opened him up to teasing by The Three Musketeers.

Hadn't one of them teased him about a blow job? Janice recalled. Girls were so forward these days. Once again Janice had to intervene to stop the ridicule that followed. She felt like a mother to him; helping him out when he got flustered on the till because a customer wanted a refund or because he was unsure where to hang the new items that had just come in. No wonder he hadn't lasted long in Electricals. Jack, the manager, would have had little patience for such an incompetent employee. Anyway, Tom just wasn't manly enough for Jack and his team, so Janice had taken him under her wing, the only male in the ladies' fashions section. She'd hoped the girls would be nice to him. Some hope!

The break over, Janice followed the others back to the shop floor.

"Tom, I want you to stay behind the till up to your lunch break," she said.

Obediently he obliged. That was the thing with him: he was *so* compliant. He did his best. He tried. Even so, Janice knew it would not be long before she had to come to his aid - and true to form within an hour he had messed up again. He had scanned a garment twice and she had to authorise the refund. She leaned over him, touching his white shirt, feeling his arm beneath hers. As she got closer to him she could smell his cheap aftershave. She exhaled heavily to make sure he felt her frustrated breath on his cheek. Felt her authority. She liked the way he blushed when he was with her, how he became flustered. It was all about power. Manipulation. And a woman's power was a lot more subtle than a man's.

"Be more careful next time," she said, when the customer had gone. Her voice was laced with authority but she wasn't sarcastic like Jack. She didn't belittle Tom. That wasn't her style at all. No, Tom liked her, she knew that, he liked being in ladies' fashions even though he was ribbed by The Three Musketeers.

He nodded shyly and muttered an apology.

The fortunate thing with Tom, Janice thought, was that her mainly female customers rarely seemed to get riled by his mistakes. Instead, they too saw the little boy lost and actually liked him and took pity on him when he made a mistake. One or two even asked who he was, with a twinkle in their matronly eyes. There was no doubt that Tom, with his blond hair, slim frame and large blue eyes would be something of a hit with the ladies - if he only realised it. But then again, his naivety was a big part of his appeal.

The following day, Janice found herself thinking about Sandra's remark about Tom being a virgin. She began to wonder whether he had ever had sex. It was clear he didn't have a girlfriend and she knew he lived at home with his mum and dad, and he came to work on a small motorbike.

Then, one Friday, when he came back from lunch, he was carrying a bag branded with a chemist shop logo.

"Got your weekend protection in there?" Janice asked mischievously.

Tom blushed. "Um, protection?"

"You know, johnnies, French letters, rubbers," Zoe teased, listing all the words she could think of for condoms.

"Oh, yeah, no, don't need them."

Zoe laughed loudly.

"Your girl on the pill, is she?" Tracey interjected.

"I've not got a girlfriend," Tom muttered.

This time Janice didn't intervene in the teasing. Instead she let Tom dig himself deeper into his hole.

"I've never kissed a girl," he confessed.

The Three Musketeers hooted with laughter. "Never kissed a girl?"

Over the following weeks, Janice watched out for Tom. Whether he was at the till or walking around the shop floor, she kept an eye on him. She took in his appearance; the unkempt blonde hair, the thin face, the slim body, the blue eyes... and shielded by the fabric of his grey or sometimes black trousers - his virgin prick.

She soon noticed that he had a habit of staring at female customers dressed in skirts, boots, leather jackets, or worse... leather skirts or trousers! What was it with the young virgin? Janice thought. When a young mother came to his till wearing a tight denim pencil skirt, black boots with three inch heels and a black leather jacket, Tom was in raptures. He even made small-talk and his eyes never left her when she walked away.

Then, on another day, a maturer lady in a leather skirt approached his till. Tom became so flustered he made a mistake and Janice had to come to his rescue; slotting her magic key into the till to overwrite the erroneous transaction. As she leant over him she looked down at his trousers and, as she suspected, they hid a large bulge. Perspiration seeped from Tom's crimson skin and she could feel his staccato breathing on her cheek.

During the afternoons, when it was quiet, she began to talk to him. She found out he had some friends with whom he went out drinking and played pool down the pub, and that he was the only one of his group without a girlfriend.

"I'm too shy around girls," he confessed.

He seemed to like talking to her though, and over the next few months Janice discovered more about him. He was lonely. Frustrated.

"It's nice to confide in someone," he said. "You're like my mother."

Janice smiled, but the next day when she was getting dressed for work she took a long hard look at herself in the mirror. OK, she was forty-nine and things were going south a little, and she was a bit plumper than she wanted to be - but hey, all women wanted to lose weight, didn't they? On the plus side she had a clear complexion and short blonde hair which always attracted the men when she went out with her friend, Diane. She certainly wasn't going to start drawing her pension yet!

She fastened her skimpy white bra over he large breasts and pulled up a pair of matching knickers; then she buttoned up her white blouse. Finally, she reached into her wardrobe and found her knee-length, black PVC skirt - the one she had occasionally worn when out for an evening. She zipped it up and added black patent, high-heeled boots.

Mother, ah, I bet his mother never dressed like this, she thought, as she looked at herself in the mirror.

Tom beamed as she walked into the staffroom.

"Janice, have you got a lover you're seeing after work?" Zoe chimed.

"Might have," Janice responded. "So mind your own."

For the rest of the day she made sure Tom feasted his eyes on her butt and breasts. She bent down in front of him so he got to see her ample breasts. She purposely leaned over him; rubbed against him so he was left in no doubt that she had an ample cleavage. Her heart raced with the thought that Tom's penis was likely to be straining against the restriction of his grey trousers, and that he might be masturbating over her in the staff toilets. And, if not there, certainly at home when he went to bed at night. He even mentioned to her that he liked her skirt.

During the afternoon tea break Sandra said to anyone who cared to listen, "Tom fancies you, Janice. He's not been able to keep his peeps off you all day!"

"I see you graduated with honours from the Saddam Hussein school of diplomacy," Janice quipped. Tom looked down at his hot chocolate, blushed, turned deepest crimson. "I'm old enough to be his mother," Janice added, to see what effect her words would have on the young man. "Well, I'm forty-nine and he's nineteen," she said, as if to labour the point. "Much too old."

Tom looked up. The expression on his face said he wasn't convinced, that if she gave him half a chance his virgin nineteen-year-old cock would like to explore some forty-something fanny.

Janice wore the tight PVC skirt again a week later and then, on the third occasion she wore it, she told Tom he needed to stay behind to help her out with an order that had just come in.

She then made up some task to keep him busy for ten minutes while the rest of the staff were leaving. When they were alone she told him to phone his mother and tell her he was going out for a drink with some of the people from work, and would not be home for dinner. She watched as he nervously flicked up his mobile phone and made the call, hesitating over the lies to his mother.

When he had finished and the shop closed for the day she said, "I think it's time you and I had a long talk, Tom. I'm not happy with your performance and how you eye-up customers - not to mention me. I think your mind is more on your cock than your work, and I want to have it out with you." She loved the innuendo - the fact that Tom was so innocent he didn't even realise what she was saying, and just blushed and muttered apologies.

"I thought we could go for a drink," Janice said. "It might be more relaxed in the pub. I always find it better to talk away from the work environment." While she spoke she rubbed her hand down her smooth PVC skirt and crossed her ankles, her eyes never leaving Tom's virgin bulge.

As Janice suspected the pub was crowded with after-work drinkers. Tom ordered a lager, which he gulped quickly, and she ordered an orange juice. They found a small table in the corner. The conversation was stilted. She felt his reticence about being alone with her.

"I'm sorry," he apologised before she had even said anything. "I won't look at customers again and I'll try to do better; I know I'm not very good."

Janice started to feel sorry for her victim. "It's not a question of not looking at women - all men like to look. It's just that you stare, particularly if you like what they're wearing. I've noticed that it's the same with me when I wear this PVC skirt. I just happened to find it in the back of the wardrobe and I've been amazed at how you stare when I wear it."

Tom's face was like a furnace. He gulped down some more lager.

"Tom, it's nothing to be ashamed of. You like women - most men do - but just try to be a little more discreet when you look at customers." She put her hand under the table and squeezed his leg. "Do I make myself clear?"

Tom nodded.

"And as for me, I'm old enough to be your mother, it's just not right that you should be lusting after me."

"I'm sorry," he said. He looked down at his drink as if he were fascinated by it. Janice wondered if there were fish swimming around the bottom of the glass.

She still held his leg, moved forward. "Here, look at me."

Tom looked up.

"You've done nothing but look at my tits and bum over the last few weeks, and I'm not particularly happy about it. I'm your boss remember, and I could have you done for sexual harassment as you've made me feel quite uncomfortable. You couldn't make it in Electricals and now you're on the verge of losing your job in my department too."

"But I like working with you," Tom protested. "Please give me another chance to prove myself. I promise not to look at you or anyone else, ever again."

Janice loved teasing him. He was like a fish caught on a fisherman's line - struggling this way and that, unaware that she was playing with him and no matter what he did he could not free himself. She would let him wriggle before she hauled him in and slapped him down over her knee.

"Do you know what I think I should do to you?" Janice said. She had played this moment over and over in her head at night, usually with a vibrator in her hand. It was the moment when she finally got to use the five letter word that carried so much power.

Tom looked up. Crimson. Confused. Awkward.

"Sack me?" he guessed.

Janice smiled. "No, spank you."

Tom was silent.

Janice continued. "I think you need your backside spanked, Tom. There you are, that's my honest opinion."

Janice watched him nervously take another swig of lager.

"I want to keep my job," Tom said. "I really do."

"Then you'll take a spanking and we'll say no more about your lust for older women," Janice said matter-of-factly.

He was like a schoolboy called to the Head's study; expecting a punishment from an adult who knew better. He was too naive to realise that Janice's clit was pulsing and that she had actually climaxed when she said the word *spank*, that she was as horny as hell.

"I get to keep my job?" Tom asked.

"Yes, after I've spanked you, we'll start again. You're off tomorrow, so when I see you at work on Monday it will be a fresh slate. You'll have a chance to start again and prove yourself. I'm only making this offer because I like you, Tom. The Three Musketeers like you too, though they have a strange way of showing it. We all want you to succeed."

He smiled. In a strange way she knew he was relieved and she wondered, not for the first time, if he had come to work each day thinking he might be sacked. He was still on probation and he knew if she reported to Personnel that he was not up to scratch then his P45 would be in the post.

Tom gripped his pint glass. "OK, I'll take a spanking," he said.

Janice tried to hide her excitement. "There's another thing. I will tell The Three Musketeers that I spanked you. I think it's important they know so they realise we're starting again. At the moment they think you're likely to be sacked. In fact, they have even taken bets on how long you'll last in ladies' fashions."

"I didn't know that," Tom said. Janice loved the lie, the drawing in of the fishing line, pulling the him closer and closer to her PVC-covered knee.

"So it's back to my place then," Janice said, draining her glass.

"What, now? Tonight?"

"There's no time like the present."

"But I thought..."

"What?"

Janice knew Tom was flustered, that he could not take in what he had just agreed to.

"I thought, well, you would perhaps do it... I dunno... at work or something."

"What? In front of The Three Musketeers? That would be worse. I said I would tell them, not show them."

Janice stood up. "Come on, we can't stay here all night. I'll drive home and you can follow on your motorbike. We won't be long."

Since her husband had moved in with her daughter-in-law's best friend she'd had the house to herself, which was how she liked it. There was no one to tell her what to do - not that Peter, her ex-husband, had ever tried to.

Janice walked to her car and waited while Tom pulled on his leather jacket and put on his helmet. When he was ready she got into her car and started the engine. As she drove she watched the mono beam of the motorbike's headlight as he followed her car back to her house. She lit a cigarette and rolled down the window. Doubts about the seduction she had so carefully planned bounced around her head. It was too late now though; she had to go through with it and the thought of spanking Tom was so all-encompassing she knew she would never be able to look at him again if she didn't do it. Anyway, hadn't he just accepted it was a fitting punishment for an incompetent employee with an eye for the well-dressed lady?

She pulled up on her drive and walked purposefully to the front door. She let herself in and took her coat off. Tom wasn't far behind. He followed her into the empty house. When he had taken off his helmet and jacket and gloves, she closed the door behind him and took his wrist. Her long nails bit into his skin. Sadistically, she tightened her grip.

"Come..."

She led him in to the front room and sat down on the dining room chair she had strategically placed in the middle of the floor that morning.

"Now, Tom," she said in her best school mistress voice, "I'm not happy with your work. Not at all. You are still on probation and we're thinking of getting rid of you. That's the truth. You'll take a spanking tonight and then we'll start again on Monday with a clean slate. Agreed?"

Tom jerked back from her grip. There were tears in his eyes. "I didn't think it would be like this."

"Agreed?"

He nodded slowly.

"And you accept that it's not only about your inability to carry out the simplest of tasks that's the problem, it is also about the way you look at customers and how you look at me. When I've worn my PVC skirt you've not been able to take your eyes off me."

"Sorry," he said. "It won't happen again."

"No, it won't happen again because I'm going to teach you a lesson, young man." Janice released his wrist and then grabbed the waistband of his trousers and pulled him forward.

"W-what's happening?" he asked. "Can't I keep my trousers on?"

"No," she insisted.

Within seconds she had undone the fastening and his trousers fell to the floor, revealing navy-blue cotton pants. She pushed them down to reveal his limp penis and two tight balls.

"Mummy's going to spank you," she said.

As he stood before her trembling, she turned up the white cotton sleeves of her blouse. Then she pulled him over her smooth knees - over the beautiful oil-slick black PVC. The white orbs of Tom's buttocks clenched and unclenched beneath her. She shifted his frame over her thighs so she had a good aim.

"Please, Janice; you can't do this to me," he pleaded. "You can't spank me. It's not right."

"OK, I tell Personnel to sack you, but I thought you had agreed..." She smacked him hard. "I thought you had agreed to take a spanking."

"I'm sorry, Janice. I know I deserve it..."

"You do deserve it and you're going to be spanked. Spanked hard."

She waited for him to reply, but he just lay over her knee quivering. When his buttocks had relaxed she delivered another stinging slap on one of the white virgin cheeks.

"Ouch," Tom squealed. He tried to put his hand up to defend his bum but Janice brushed it away. She walloped him with a third slap on the other cheek.

Tom's yell was stifled by a fourth, fifth and sixth smack. Flesh on flesh; Janice's motherly hand beating out a rhythm on the smooth boyish bum. He wriggled and raised his hand and told her to stop, but Janice knew he accepted her authority and his punishment.

"I would stop struggling and raising your hand," she ordered. "I'm going to spank you whether you like it or not." She swept her hand down on his squirming buttocks: seven, eight, nine more times.

"Please stop!" Tom whimpered. "Why are you doing this to me?"

"Because you are an incompetent, useless excuse of a young man who gets a hard-on when he sees a female in a tight skirt." Janice smacked his bottom again and again and again as she spoke. Smack, smack, smack. Soon a lovely rosy hue was drifting across the beaten cheeks. His backside was as red as his face when The Three Musketeers teased him.

Tom seemed to give in to his fate as he stopped struggling and lay still over her lap. Janice took a deep breath and eased up on her initial volley of smacks. Her pussy was wet; she had been waiting so long for this moment there was no way Tom would be released until she had spanked him properly. She loved the feel of him laying over her knee, not struggling, not being spanked but just lying there. So after the first volley she let him rest, then chided him, spanked him, let him lie still, then chided him, spanked him, let him lie still. That was the pattern.

As the time ticked by her mind turned to thoughts of disciplinary tribunals and instant dismissal for gross misconduct. You just weren't allowed to do this to an employee - not even to one as useless as Tom. But then she'd made sure the incident had taken place outside work in her own home, after Tom had agreed to accept a spanking. Not that Tom would complain, she knew. She delivered another stinging rebuke to the soft white skin. And another.

"Stop," he cried limply.

As if in answer Janice gave the beaten cheeks another couple of hearty smacks. And all the while Tom's cock grew harder as it rubbed against her skirt, jerked forward by the violent smacks. The sensation of the hard stalk on her thigh aroused her. His juices leaked onto the shiny black of her skirt, creating a lubricant.

"I'm sorry," he blustered. "I'll do better. Honest. I won't look at anyone ever again. Stop now, please."

"You bet you'll do better and you'll stop ogling the female customers," Janice chided as she beat a quick rhythmic tattoo on each buttock.

When the orbs had taken on a splendid red hue she stopped. She had never felt so alive. So excited. So turned on. She pushed him off her knee. He fell to the carpet and rolled onto his back, stretched out, eyes closed, panting hard. Cock to attention. A sensation of utter domination and control ran through Janice's veins. She tore off her blouse, hitched up her skirt and slipped off her knickers. She then lowered her pussy so that his standing projectile made contact with her sex lips. Easing the mouth of her vagina over his cock, she eased it up inside her. Ecstasy. Pure ecstasy. She had never felt so turned on. Pete, for all his womanising and experience, had not been able to turn her on as much as the virgin Tom. As his cock filled her she let herself go and collapsed onto the stiff piston. Tom groaned with delight as, for the first time ever, his penis found its way inside a woman. Janice was astride him like an experienced horsewoman on an unbridled pony. She moved back and forth on his erection, mastering his cock. His immature hands gripped her large breasts as she rode him. He squirmed and writhed beneath her.

All too quickly a great load exploded into Janice. Her vagina tightened around his cock, held it in its vicelike grip as she too orgasmed.

"Oh God!" she gasped as one rapturous wave of pleasure after another rolled over her. She had never had sex like it.

"Oh! Wicked!" Tom exclaimed. "That was well wicked! I love you, Janice. Oh my God! Fuck me, I love you, Janice. I love you!"

His crimson face shone with a smile of utter contentment.

Janice fell forward and stared into his large blue eyes. She pinned his wrists to the carpet. She panted, exhausted, exhilarated.

"How does it feel, my little lost virgin? How does it feel to be seduced by an older woman?" She laughed. "I'm thirty years older than you." She pressed her lips to his and massaged her breasts against his chest. The warmth of his body radiated into hers, and she felt his semi-limp cock flop against her thigh.

"Let's go to bed," she said. "Phone your mother and tell her you're at your girlfriend's house. That'll surprise her."

Tom got up and took his mobile from his trousers, then once again he made the call to his mother. Then Janice led him up to bed, where this time she let Tom go on top of her. He pumped away earnestly as she held on to his red warm bum.

"Twice in one night, you awful womaniser," she teased, as they lay together afterwards.

"Thanks, Janice," he muttered. "I won't forget this."

"Of course you won't, Tom," she said. "I'll make sure of that."

She knew he would not be so bashful around the Three Musketeers in future. He might even pluck up the courage to ask Sandra out; Janice knew she fancied him.

"Now, get dressed and go home to your real mother, and I'll see you at work on Monday. Bright and early. And no more mistakes, do you hear, or you'll be back over my knee."

Tom slipped on his clothes as she pulled on a negligee. Then he went back to the hall and collected his helmet, gloves and coat. She kissed him goodnight at the front door and he walked out to his motorbike.

As soon as he'd roared away she booted up her computer and accessed her Facebook page. She knew The Three Musketeers were on her friendship list, so what better way to tell them about the evening she'd had? That she'd just spanked young Tom's arse and taken his virginity. Now that really would be something for Zoe, Sandra and Tracey, collectively known as The Three Musketeers, to tease him about on Monday morning.

CHASTISING CARA
The Boyfriend's Tale

Andrew Hanson stood over the toilet basin, his flaccid cock in his large hand. His heart vibrated against his ribcage. He could hardly contain himself. This time Cara was going to get a spanking. A real spanking. A deserved, punishment spanking.

He had needed to come upstairs to the bathroom to calm down and compose himself before he committed the assault. He smiled as he thought of his girlfriend downstairs in his bedsit blissfully unaware of the sadomasochistic thoughts running through his head... unaware of the scene about to be played out... unaware that all afternoon he had been planning the punishment Cara was to receive...

He had met Cara at work - a small firm of solicitors called Cliff and Sons. He had been twenty-four and an up and coming legal graduate with a promising career in front of him. She had been twenty, a small, slim, big-busted secretary who typed up his letters. He asked her out and soon a relationship flourished. At first it had been like all his previous relationships, but gradually he noticed that Cara expected him to take the lead and make decisions. Andrew slowly pushed the boundaries, suggesting what she might like to wear or choosing food for her when they went out to a restaurant. It had surprised him that Cara always ceded to his wishes - usually with a polite, thin-lipped smile and a glint in her green eyes. Occasionally though, when she'd not wished to do something but had done it all the same, she made her feelings felt with a caustic or sarcastic response which annoyed him but showed that there was still something wild within her that needed to be tamed. And that excited him.

Her most regular rebukes were, "You always know what's best for me." Or, "You're always trying to protect me." And the one Andrew particularly enjoyed hearing when it came to sex, "You just help yourself."

Mostly, however, she accepted the lead Andrew took without a murmur. She even admitted she was old-fashioned and liked a man to be in charge. Andrew enjoyed his domination of Cara, the fact she looked up to him and seemed dependent upon him; he felt like a man. A real man. A man from the Hollywood movies of the Thirties and Forties.

As the relationship developed Andrew began to notice there was not much depth to Cara. His best friend described her as a thick secretary with big tits, and though the judgement was a little harsh it was nonetheless accurate, for she had little personality and her only conversation seemed to revolve around make-up, fashions and pop groups. Andrew realised fairly early on that she would never become Mrs Hanson; a lifetime of such banal chatter would have surely driven him to despair. But what intrigued him was the submissive role she played and how she bestowed upon him some mysterious power as if he were her appointed master. She didn't much like her secretarial role at Cliff and Sons, so he had updated her CV for her and sent it out. Eventually she was offered some interviews and Andrew had taken her shopping and bought her some suitable suits to wear. Then despite her best efforts to mess up her interviews, eventually she was offered another, better paid job.

"Andrew, you're my hero!" she had said, and proceeded to wrap her arms around his neck when she received the good news that she'd landed a new job as a PA. She kissed him passionately as if he had just predicted the winning numbers in a lottery. Andrew smiled smugly; Cara had become a little more under his control.

Andrew's motivation for getting Cara another job had not been altogether altruistic. He wanted her out of Cliffs. He knew his peers and bosses were rather surprised at his choice for a girlfriend, and he always found it embarrassing when he saw her at work and had to talk to her in a business fashion when everyone knew he and Cara were an item. Also he, feeling no long term commitment to her, wanted to play the field, and a clingy girlfriend at work was too much to handle. For the first time he had a place of his own as he had rented a flat as soon as he started at Cliffs, and he was determined to enjoy his freedom. Cara was his third girlfriend since leaving university three years previously, and he knew she would not be his last.

Andrew finished his toilet and washed his clammy hands. His breathing had returned to something equating to normal, but still he felt a blissful tingling down his spine. He tried to repress the words but they bounced and spun around his head: *Cara Rosetti was going to get a spanking. Cara Rosetti was going to get a spanking.* He took ten deep breaths. Composure, composure, composure, he told himself.

If it was her submissive side that had drawn Andrew in, it was her responses to his rebukes that really turned him on. Like any couple they'd had their disagreements and, when he got annoyed one day and shouted at her, instead of the spirited response he had always received from his previous girlfriends, he was met with a meek apology from Cara. It seemed she expected to be told off, and like an errant child, accepted her scolding without rebellion. Andrew found himself telling her off more and more and for smaller and smaller slights, and each time the response from her was the same: she was sorry, sometimes tearfully sorry, but always sorry. Her compunctious nature also lead her to send Andrew cards and letters with further apologies for real and imagined misdemeanours she had committed over the weekend.

The weekend. That was the thing. Cara lived at home with her Italian parents, who had a somewhat old-fashioned attitude to raising children. Her mother was a particularly formidable lady who did not like Andrew; he was not of her church and he was leading Cara astray. To satisfy her mother and boyfriend Cara arranged only to see him at weekends, and he was perhaps not as upset as he might have been by this arrangement. A fellow law graduate, Alison, was showing more than a professional interest in him and he was determined to develop that relationship as well. She was well aware of Cara and didn't seem to mind his dalliance with the big-busted law firm secretary. So, mid-weeks belonged to Alison, and weekends belonged to Cara.

Andrew enjoyed his weekends. He would collect Cara from her parents' house on a Friday night and drop her back home on a Sunday, so that Cara went from her mother's control to her boyfriend's control with seamless ease, each taking it in turns to hold the reins.

Andrew placed a foot on the stair. While in the bathroom he had not heard any noise from any of the other three rented rooms in the house, and guessed all the other occupants were out. His bedsit was at the back of the house, the only room downstairs, and next to it was a little used communal sitting room. It was Saturday afternoon and all was quite, and not for the first time he regretted surrendering his flat, but his finances had become stretched due to juggling two girlfriends. Still, needs must, he told himself, and the privacy of the bedsit still allowed him the opportunity to rebuke Cara.

He wasn't sure if it was because of her Italian origin but, allied to Cara's immature nature, on occasions she threw childish tantrums. The first time Andrew had witnessed a tantrum they had been to a party: Cara had looked particularly stunning, but when they returned to Andrew's flat she had thrown a tantrum.

"I don't like those stupid people!" she exclaimed, talking about his friends. "They're all so full of themselves and that stupid Nigel took the rise out of me because I didn't know who Guy Fawkes was or what Spaghetti Junction was. They're stupid, stupid people. I don't like them and I'm not going to that stupid Christina's wedding either, so there!"

Andrew had been open-mouthed. Stunned. Cara, normally so submissive, could also be fiery and temperamental, could she?

The next time she threw a tantrum he slapped her face.

Maybe a month later Andrew took her to see some university friends of his, who were still living in the student lodgings close to the old red brick Northern university he had attended. It was a long trip up North. He had wanted to take Alison with him and tried to put Cara off with tales of the long journey and the early start, but she insisted - she was, after all, his girlfriend and she wanted to meet his friends.

They had arrived mid-afternoon and he introduced her to the two couples, thereafter feeling rather self-conscious of his choice in girlfriends. For while the others talked about careers and politics, Cara sat quietly unable to join in and, when every once in a while one of his friends' female partners asked her a purposefully probing question, Andrew was usually left feeling embarrassed by the reply and a feeling that things would have been so much better if he had been firmer and insisted she did not come with him, which would have meant he would have been able to take Alison instead. But that was the problem, Andrew considered; he was just too soft when it came to Cara.

That night they were allocated a small room with a single bed. Before they went out Cara had tied her hair back and dressed in a tight skirt and her usual high heels. She looked incongruous in comparison with the other girls, who wore DMs and cargo trousers. After a meal and a pub crawl they returned to their lodgings and chatted - all except Cara, who sat dutifully on Andrew's knee.

Inevitably, a joint had started to do the rounds and much to Cara's annoyance Andrew took a drag. When they returned to their small room Cara wasn't talking, so Andrew settled down and went to sleep. Sometimes he got thoroughly annoyed with her childishness and her silent moods, when he did things she didn't like.

In the middle of the night he awoke. He heard a rustling noise and could see a movement in the darkened room. He blinked to focus. Cara. He watched her for a few minutes. She was dressed in jeans, trainers and a jumper, and was packing her bag.

"What are you doing?" he asked.

"I'm leaving," Cara spat. "I'm not sleeping here in this dump. The sheets are dirty and I'm not staying with a load of dope-heads!"

Andrew could not believe it. He looked at his watch.

"But its three a.m.! You don't know anyone in this town," he hissed.

"I'll go to a hotel."

"Nothing will be open. Now get into bed and don't be so childish."

"No."

Andrew felt his temper rising. "Cara, get undressed and get into bed before I spank you!"

The words had an almost magical effect. Cara dropped her bag and slowly started to undo her jeans and pull off her T-shirt. Moments later she was back in bed. Andrew got on top of her, his cock rock-hard. He hadn't felt like sex when they got into bed, but now wide awake he felt really turned on - and those magic words seemed to turn her on as much as they did him, for her pussy was moist and inviting. Within seconds he was pounding his large horn into her as she squeaked and squealed excitedly.

"You narrowly avoided a spanking there, Cara," he said as he at last withdrew his well-pleasured cock.

A few weeks later there had been the nightclub incident. At the time Andrew was serving time on his downstairs flat. As he was Cara's first boyfriend she seemed to enjoy the advances of other men as it was something she had never experienced before - especially as Andrew had taught her to dress in a provocative way. Hence, she would often go out wearing a miniskirt and tight top to show off her ample assets - frequently without any underwear. On this particular occasion she wore skyscraper heels, a black leather mini and a tight white top. Predictably she had received the attention she craved, particularly from a young admirer who had taken the liberty of chatting her up while Andrew went to the toilet. He came back to see her engaged in conversation with the young stud, who quickly disappeared when Andrew reappeared.

"He touched my bum," Cara said, as Andrew approached.

"Why didn't you tell him to get lost?"

She didn't have a reply, and he knew she enjoyed the attention. When they got back to his flat he challenged her again about her flirting. As usual she threw a tantrum and stalked off to the bathroom, Andrew behind her. He grabbed her arm and pushed her over the basin with one hand, and at the same time brought his free hand down on her black leather skirt with a heavy thud. Slap, smack, slap. His right hand beat out a healthy tattoo on the black leather. Andrew made sure Cara's flirting was punished, and afterwards he was well aware that her backside stung. She shouted at him to stop but he made sure he gave her six solid wallops - he then walked out of the bathroom and went to bed.

A while later Cara came to the bedroom wearing a silky rose-coloured negligee.

"That hurt," she said, rubbing her backside. Andrew watched as her two hands moved the silk of the negligee up and down her buttocks to indicate how sore her two orbs were. His cock stood to attention.

"You deserved it," he said.

As soon as she was in bed he was on top of her again, his erection entering her wet cunt, pushing deep. It was without doubt one of the best nights of lovemaking he'd had. He just wished Alison could turn him on as much as Cara did.

A few weeks later... another nightclub... another repeat of Cara's flirting... another spanking in the bathroom. Something told him she enjoyed misbehaving and being punished.

Then there was the incident at the seaside resort on the August bank holiday weekend. Once again Cara wore a belt-like miniskirt and ensnared a young man into flirting with her. This time they were staying in a bed and breakfast, so when they left the nightclub Andrew had to think on his feet. After a brief exchange of words he turned his girlfriend over the wall of the esplanade and proceeded to give her a few hearty smacks as waves lapped against the stone fortifications and onlookers watched, amazed and excited.

Then his tenure on the flat had expired. It had proved too expensive to maintain so he had to move into a bedsit in a shared house. His freedom was curtailed - until that fateful Saturday afternoon...

He stepped off the last stair and walked the few feet to his room. He passed the empty communal room, then pushed open the door of his own room. It was small but compact. To his left was a single bed onto which Cara had thrown her black leather jacket and her handbag. A few bags of shopping sat beside the basin, which had a vanity shield next to it. Then there was an expanse of wall, an armchair, a TV in the corner under a small window, and then the kitchenette area, which comprised cupboards on the walls, a sink and drainer, cooker and small fridge. Cara stood at the sink peeling potatoes. The television was on. Andrew listened to the light plop as a potato fell into a saucepan on the stove. The sleeves of her white jumper were rolled up, her long black hair was in a ponytail and hung down her back. Then there was the pert bottom encased in a black skirt. The high-heeled boots added a kinky dimension to the ensemble. Against the wall on his immediate right was a dining table and two chairs. Cara had placed some mats, cutlery and condiments upon it. Andrew did not feel hungry.

He dropped the latch on the door. No one could enter. It had been a long time since he had spoken to Cara and he wondered if he should perhaps say something. He knew she would be aware by now that he was in the room, but she chose to ignore him; pretending, no doubt, that the TV was covering his presence.

He paused. On the floor in front of him were his slippers. He kicked one ahead of him. It landed under the table. He walked further into the room...

The day had started badly. It was the last Saturday before Christmas and Mrs Rossetti had wanted to go shopping with Cara. Andrew would have been more than happy with a weekend off - perhaps a few pints with friends and a trip to Alison's flat in the afternoon. But Cara's mum couldn't drive, nor could Cara, and Mr Rossetti was elsewhere. So he was called upon to be the taxi service. Taking Cara and her mum to a large out of town shopping centre the weekend before Christmas was not his idea of a fun-filled day, but he duly obliged, not having any suitable excuse available.

They had arrived at the shopping mall and parked up. Cara and her mum walked off in front of him and began to investigate the shops. Andrew waited and waited while Cara and her mum took ages to decide what to buy in each shop - then, for his sins, he got to carry the bags.

"I think this would look lovely on the mantelpiece at home," Cara said, about a Christmas decoration.

"No, it's too fussy."

"Oh, isn't this adorable?" Cara said about something else.

"I don't like it," Mrs Rossetti's said.

And so it went on. Andrew felt like a proverbial spare prick and amused himself by watching Cara bend over in her tight skirt; even so, to all intents and purposes he was persona no grata - Mrs Rossetti still had hold of the reins and Andrew knew that where her mother was concerned Cara was always subservient and put her mother first. He was a distant second.

That's why the events that unfolded took him completely by surprise. Cara and her mother had left one shop clearly annoyed with each other.

"You're getting too big for your boots," he heard Mrs Rossetti say. His ears pricked up, but he still missed most of the rat-a-tat-tat spitfire exchange of verbal gunfire between mother and daughter, which ended with Cara telling her mum to "fuck off", before she turned on her high heels and stalked off.

Passers-by had stopped and stared briefly, and then continued their shopping - by which time Cara had been absorbed into the crowd. Mrs Rossetti had been unfazed. She turned around and walked towards another shop - Andrew in close attendance. He had no idea where Cara had gone, so dutifully he followed Mrs Rossetti around the shops for the rest of the trip and then trudged back to the car loaded up with her shopping bags. Cara was waiting, perched against the bonnet.

Neither spoke to her. When Mrs Rossetti and her shopping had been deposited back at her house she only said a curt goodbye to Andrew. Cara moved into the passenger seat and had attempted to engage him in conversation as they drove off, but Andrew remained silent. He hadn't wanted to waste his Saturday shopping, and now this - he was too good-natured.

They arrived back at the bedsit and almost immediately he ran upstairs to the toilet...

He was behind her now. She still didn't turn. He took a deep breath. It was now or never. He had fantasised about this moment, masturbated over it - Cara doing something that really enraged him and met by stern, old-fashioned discipline. She knew he was there but she chose to ignore him. Perhaps she hoped he was going to kiss her, but it wasn't to be. Suddenly he grabbed her arm around the bicep. A surge of power ran through him, as if making a connection with his submissive victim had supercharged him. He felt a sense of injustice; Cara and her mother had treated him badly and it was payback time, for the truth was he was seething with rage. He was absolutely furious with Cara - despite his errant cock believing he was acting out an erotic scene. He knew he wanted to punish her - not just for the spectacle she had made of herself in the shopping mall, but for all the times she had let him down with her careless, idiotic chatter; all the times she had made inane comments that had been overheard and led to their collective embarrassment; all the times she had demonstrated her ignorance at the top of her voice. He wanted to punish her. Good and hard. God, did he want to punish her.

He pulled her. Pulled her round. She was forced to look at him. He wide green eyes sparkled, questioned, wondered. She knew she had done wrong. There was a look of fear on her face, a look of penitence. Andrew knew that was why she had got straight on with the dinner, but that was not enough. He wanted punishment, revenge, retribution.

He dragged her back. Her hands were wet from peeling the potatoes and she still held the peeler in one hand.

"What, what are you doing?" she half asked, half pleaded.

Andrew hissed through gritted teeth. "I'm going to punish you, young lady. Punish you like you've never before been punished."

Cara's breathing was staccato. "I'm sorry," she said. "You know what she's like."

It was a desperate bid to get him to take her side, to make him agree that Mrs Rossetti was a dominating ogre who had deserved to be challenged so aggressively in a public place. But Andrew wasn't falling for that. On this occasion his sympathies were firmly with Mrs Rossetti. The adult.

"No, I don't know what she's like, but I know what you're like and you've overstepped the mark this time, and you're going to get a proper spanking, which will do you no end of good."

"You can't... I mean... I'm sorry... we were arguing over you... mum said you looked bored and sullen... I was defending you..."

Andrew smiled. The minx was good, he would give her that.

"You're nothing but a spoilt brat, Cara. You know how your mother used to smack your bottom with a hairbrush? Well, this is going to be like that."

"But I'm twenty years old!" she pleaded.

"Well, behave like it!" he blasted.

During the exchange he manoeuvred one of the dining chairs out so it was away from the table. His grip on her arm became tighter. He sat down and pulled Cara over his knee. She struggled. He grasped both her wrists in one hand and forced them up her back. She squealed. Pleaded. Her ponytail flopped about her head. Her tight black skirt stretched over her pert buttocks. Andrew reached down to the floor and picked up the conveniently placed slipper, then holding it by the heel he brought it down with an almighty *thwack!* Cara yelled and kicked out her feet but unfortunately the proximity of the table to the chair meant she only kicked its underside. The noise of heel on wood reverberated through the room. Her feet were entrapped. Andrew walloped her again and again with the slipper and each time Cara squealed and wriggled and cried. After ten blows he dropped the slipper, but the punishment wasn't over. Far from it.

He caressed her buttocks, enjoying how they flinched as his hand rolled over them, fearing further swats. He took hold of the waistband. There was no time for niceties so with a quick jerk he tore down Cara's expensive skirt. A button pinged into the air and landed on the floor, the zip burst and the lifeless material slipped down Cara's legs to serve its last useful purpose - as a further binding for her thrashing feet.

"My skirt!" she exclaimed.

"Is the least of your worries."

She was wearing tights. Underneath Andrew could make out the silky blue of her knickers. Cara always did like expensive lingerie. He grabbed the hem of the tights and knickers as one and pulled them down to expose her bare buttocks.

"Enough now; this has gone too far," Cara said, as if she was somehow in control.

"Not nearly far enough," he countered.

The virgin orbs were white and tender as the slipper had, as Andrew suspected, made little impact. He clenched and unclenched his hand before raising it and bringing down the hard palm upon her left buttock. Cara yelped. Andrew did the same on the right cheek. Cara yelped again and screamed for him to stop. She kicked out madly against the table as if beating a drum to a four/four beat. Andrew had only just started. Soon he was building up a rhythm: left, right, left, right. Spank, spank, spank. It was almost mechanical and his throbbing hand was certainly making an impact, the virgin orbs taking on a rosy hue as his right hand beat and beat Cara's buttocks. This wasn't six or ten short smacks in the bathroom over a leather skirt; this was a good old-fashioned spanking and Andrew felt rather pleased with himself.

On the stove the potatoes started to boil. On the TV a scientist was pontificating about the perils of global warming. Orb warming, Andrew thought. His palm was leaving an impressive imprint. The buttocks were turning different hues of crimson, red, pink, burgundy, cherry. Occasionally Cara's head bobbed up and down, but by and large she took the punishment meekly. She sobbed, she yelped, but she took the punishment bravely.

Until Andrew returned to the slipper. He picked it up off the floor and walloped Cara with as much force as his tiring arm could muster. He knew he had lost it; a man possessed, beating his girlfriend until his arm ached and his lust was uncontrollable.

"That hurts!" she sobbed between tears. "That really, really, really hurts."

Andrew didn't answer, he wanted to save his breath for the punishment, he was oblivious to her sobs. With one last almighty smack he beat her bottom and dropped the slipper. Cara remained over his knee, her breasts heaving, sobbing, tears falling upon the carpet.

Andrew could wait no longer. He hauled her to her knees and then to her feet. She looked a pitiful wretch. Her mascara had run, her face was blotchy and her tights and skirt were around her ankles. He dragged her to the bed. He threw her down on top of her leather coat and handbag and unbuckled his trousers. Seconds later he was on top of her. His cock was fit to bursting as he eased it into Cara's sex.

"You deserved it, didn't you?" he whispered, when he was fully immersed.

She murmured in agreement, her welcoming cunt accepting him as he sank his throbbing cock into her. He probed deeper and deeper, her vagina tightening around him. Andrew withdrew and stabbed again. He knew she had enjoyed the punishment and that whoever she settled down with would have a very hard act to follow.

"You beat the living daylights out of me," she gasped as her mouth found his. "It's what I needed."

Andrew probed deeper before ejaculating inside her, her vagina milking his stiff rod as she squealed in ecstasy. Her body shivered involuntarily as she climaxed in unison with him, their bodies coupled together in unrivalled bliss.

"The potatoes have boiled dry," he said, as he pulled up his trousers.

"I don't feel like eating," she murmured dreamily.

"I bet you don't. I'll go and get a pizza and we can have it with a bottle of wine. Then you can do your homework."

"Homework?"

"Yes, I want you to write a letter of apology to your mum. You can tell her how you were punished tonight and how sorry you are. Then we can deliver it to her when I drop you off tomorrow."

"Andrew, no!" Cara protested.

"Andrew, yes. Now you don't want another spanking, do you? Well, do you?"

SANTA SPANKER
The Employee's Tale

Santa Claus was pissed off. He pulled down his elasticated white beard and took a slurp of bottled water. God, it was hot in the costume. Outside the grotto he could hear the elves entertaining the children - soon another snotty-nosed little brat would be sitting at his side and delving into his sack of cheap presents.

Footsteps approached. Frank - aka Santa - snapped his beard back into place.

"Ho! Ho! Ho!" he guffawed as a child entered the grotto; he tried to be as jocular as possible. "Do you want to see what Santa has for you?" Frank asked the boy. The lad knelt at Frank's feet as his obese mother hovered over him.

It was the usual routine. A few questions and answers like *have you been a good kid?* And, *what do you want for Christmas?* - just so all concerned felt they were getting their monies' worth. Richardson insisted that each "audience with Santa", as he liked to call it, lasted two minutes. No more, no less.

I wouldn't mind betting he's got one of the elves timing me, Frank thought.

Frank had been doing the job for years. Normally he worked in the accounts department of Jacobs department store but, because of his size, some years previously he'd volunteered to play Santa Claus. At the time it had seemed new and fun, but that was eight years ago and now he was fed up with it. He knew Richardson didn't like him and took a sadistic pleasure in ensuring that whenever the moth-eaten Santa outfit came out of storage it was Frank who got to wear it. And every year Frank told Richardson it was the last time. Period. Yet somehow Richardson always contrived to find a way of ensuring that Frank got the "Santa gig" - as he termed it - as if it had somehow been added to his job description.

The child looked downcast at his tacky present as he took his mother's fat hand and wandered through the exit. It was worse this year, Frank reflected. Richardson had planned the Christmas party to coincide with Frank's grotto duties, so whilst all the other staff in accounts were down the bar getting drunk as a prelude to the office party frolics to follow, he was sitting in his Santa grotto like a proverbial spare prick. It was the final straw; Frank had written his letter of resignation and left it on Richardson's desk. That would teach the smuck a lesson. Who would get the "Santa gig" then?

Frank guessed the lad with the roly-poly mother was his last customer of the day, as he could hear the elves chatting amongst themselves, the vertically challenged little mischief-makers. There were two of them, hired each year by Richardson from a theatre agency and, in slack times, they took great pleasure in testing Frank's patience, teasing him and running off with his things.

Frank loosened his beard again and took another swig of water. The beard irritated his skin and made him sweat.

He was berating his bad luck when, all of a sudden, outside the grotto, he heard the clip, clip, clop of high-heeled shoes. Moments later a blonde mane bent forward and ducked through the narrow gap which was the entrance to the plastic cave. Tanya. Frank's eyes lit up. She was Richardson's new PA and one of the only good reasons for working for the store. She stretched up to her full height and stood before him. She was wearing a short, cherry-coloured mac that revealed a tiny red leather miniskirt, and red stilettos were pinned to the bottom of her long, tanned legs.

"This is my Christmas outfit - do you like it?" she asked.

"Stunning," Frank said. "Has the party started?"

"Oh, no, they're still down the bar. They'll be back soon though. I just thought I'd come and see how you're doing, Frankie."

She took off her mac and sat on Frank's knee. She ran a dangerously sharp red nail down his cheek. He could smell alcohol on her breath; it blended with her perfume and hair spray to create an intoxicating mix.

"Richardson up to his old tricks, is he?" Frank asked.

Tanya nodded. Richardson liked to think he was God's gift and had had his eye on Tanya for ages. As far as Frank knew she had resisted his advances.

"I just wanted to get away from that sleazeball," she moaned. "I thought this would be the one place he wouldn't come looking for me." She paused. "They'll be finished in the bar soon, and then they'll be back in the accounts office for the party. I don't want to get lumbered with Richardson all night."

Frank could feel his cock rapidly rising beneath the red Santa gown. Surely Tanya's leather-clad buttocks could feel it?

She leaned closer to Frank, almost resting her head on his shoulder. He could feel the warmth of her body, the softness of her large breasts, and the smell of the shampoo in her hair. Her erect nipples pushed against the white nylon of her top. God, Frank felt hot, his erection killing him. When Tanya left he would have to relieve himself. Elves or no elves, he needed a wank. Then he had second thoughts. Was Tanya Webb coming on to him? Women normally steered well clear - especially those as beautiful as Tanya.

"Santa, baby..." she sung seductively in a Marilyn Monroe-ish voice, drawing a red fingernail under his chin. "What have you got in your sack for me?"

"Um, that depends," Frank blurted.

"On what?"

"Whether you've been a good girl or not. Santa only gives presents to kids who've been good."

Frank was pleased Tanya could not see him blushing behind his beard. He felt stupid; why was he using his Santa patter on the leggy twenty-four year old? Why was he treating her like a child? She had come to the grotto to seduce him and he was so fazed by it the only things he could think of saying were the corny lines he said to six year olds. He was surprised when Tanya played along.

"What would happen if I'd been a naughty girl?" she asked.

"Well, that would depend on just how naughty you've been, but you wouldn't get any presents for a kick off." Again Frank berated himself for being so inept at chat-up lines. Who would want the cheap Chinese-made shite he had in his sack? Even the kids turned their noses up when they unwrapped their presents - one spoilt brat had even thrown his toy car back in Frank's face.

"I've got a little confession to make," Tanya said. "I know I can tell you because no one talks to you down here, and even when you're in accounts you keep yourself to yourself and no one seems to bother you much."

"Case of having to," Frank said. He lived alone in a bedsit, read cheap pulp fiction thrillers and went to the bookies every week for a bet on the horses. That was it. Oh, and there were occasional trips to a massage parlour for a bit of light relief.

"I know I can trust you, Frankie - can I trust you?" Tanya asked. As if to emphasise the point she gave him a gentle kiss on the lips. Then another. She crossed her legs as she sat on his bulky knee and kicked her red shoes in the air.

"You can trust me, Tanya," he said. He cock was rock hard under the red gown. She could certainly trust that, he thought.

"I've been really, really naughty, Frankie, but please don't judge me."

Frank wondered where all this was going. Surely, Tanya in her semi-inebriated state, had not mistaken the red of the Santa outfit for the black of a priest's habit? He felt like a priest in a confessional.

"Why? What have you done?"

Tanya was coy. "If I tell you, promise me you won't tell anyone else, and I don't mind if you do punish me just an itsy bitsy tiny bit because I have been a naughty girl. But if you do punish me then not too much."

"I promise," Frank said. He was beginning to get bored with the whole charade. What had started as erotic had been deflated by his ham chat-up lines and Tanya's need to confess to a sin as yet undisclosed.

She ran her finger down his cheek. "You're the only one I can tell and I need to tell someone."

"What have you done?" Frank asked.

"I don't know... I mean, how to tell you... I mean, you hate him so much... and well... I feel such a whore." She flicked her blonde mane.

Frank knew the awful Richardson was involved. Somehow that slimeball had wormed his way into Tanya's affections.

"I've sucked Dennis Richardson's cock," she blurted without preamble.

Frank was flabbergasted. If he had not been sitting down he would have fallen over. His first thought was to push Tanya off his knee. He could not stand that arsehole Richardson, and to think Tanya's lips had been on his *thing* - those glorious ruby-red lips had sucked Richardson's tool. It was too much - especially as those same lips had kissed him!

"That really is naughty," Frank murmured. "Far worse than I had ever imagined. How did it happen?"

Tanya started to relate the whole sordid tale - Richardson had been trying it on ever since she started, pestering her for sex, flirting, making suggestive remarks.

"Sometimes I think he only appointed me for my body," Tanya admitted.

Frank didn't like to say anything, but he knew she was correct - from what he knew about her she was well organised and competent at her job, but she was certainly no better than the po-faced Mrs Rothschild who had left under a cloud of suspicion. All ways round appointing a competent piece of eye candy had been a good move by Richardson.

"So how come you sucked his jammy dodger?" Frank asked.

"Well, I made a mistake. I organised a meeting and forgot to tell the key speaker when the meeting was so the meeting was pointless. Apparently some top blokes came down from head office and it made Richardson look a fool."

"Not hard," Frank said.

Tanya smiled, syrupy sweet. She continued. "Richardson threatened me with a disciplinary and I just burst into tears and said I was really sorry and I would do anything..."

Frank could guess the rest. Richardson had taken advantage of the distraught Tanya and demanded she draw down his zipper and release his cock. Apparently it had happened in the office the other day. Since then Richardson saw no reason why she should not repeat the performance whenever he asked. Tanya was in a great big hole.

"And what with the economic climate the way it is," she went on. "Jobs are in short supply and if I don't give in to the leach I know he'll make my life a misery."

"You could take him to a tribunal... do him for sexual harassment."

"Yeah, right," Tanya sneered. "Who's going to believe my word against his?"

Frank knew she had a point. She had a reputation for being a bit flirtatious - as his knees would testify - and probably couldn't help herself. Either way the women didn't like her, probably because they were jealous, and the men wanted to shag her. In short, she was between a rock and a hard place.

Frank thought back to his letter of resignation. Maybe he would get Tanya to take it off Richardson's desk. He would stay with the store for a while longer while he decided how to take on the malevolent Richardson. Meanwhile, Tanya really believed she deserved a punishment for her antics in the office, and he was not about to persuade her otherwise.

"I know I shouldn't have done it," she said. "I feel such a fool now. I can't say anything as I've given into Richardson once and he's got me over a barrel. Please help me Frankie; you're the only one I can turn to."

Frank thought for a moment. "I am going to have to punish you, Tanya," he said. "Richardson was wrong to compromise you in the way he did, but a pretty girl like you must be used to propositions and you should have resisted. My guess is you quite liked it in a masochistic kinda way."

Tanya nodded her blonde mane. "There was certainly something a bit thrilling about doing it in the office," she admitted.

"Therefore, I'm going to punish you," Frank repeated.

"How?" she asked.

"I'm going to spank you." Frank's cock had deflated, but on speaking the magic words it immediately jumped back to attention. Tanya looked aghast.

"When I said punish me, I was only joking," she backtracked. "I just said it as I didn't know how to tell you about what I had done, and it seemed the easiest thing to say especially as you play the big Father Christmas role."

"No matter. You deserve to be punished and you will be punished." With a well-practiced grab of her arm Frank pulled Tanya over his knee, her leather-clad bum wriggling seductively. It was quiet in the mall and Frank guessed the elves had gone and the store was closed; bar the party in the back offices - the party he wasn't invited to. No, he knew he would be undisturbed for the next ten minutes or so, by which time Tanya's pert young bum would be well and truly spanked.

He manoeuvred her into position, and then he brought his heavy hand down onto Tanya's bum with a loud whack. She squealed and tried to defend her backside with her other hand.

"No, Frankie, this has gone too far, I only told you because I thought I could trust you, I never seriously wanted to be punished," she rambled.

"But you've had Richardson's cock in your mouth and that deserves a spanking,"

Frank said. "You're a little tart, and your arse is going to feel it tonight."

He grabbed her wrists and held them both in his left hand, as he did so he raised his right again and swept it down with a reverberating smack. He loved the sound of flesh on leather - the impact it made. The way the noise echoed around the artificial grotto walls. He never got much for Christmas, but this was one present that would live in his memory for a long, long time. He walloped her again. And again.

"Ouch! Stop now, Frankie," Tanya begged, but he was in no mood for stopping; having a beautiful girl over his knee was the pinnacle of all his fantasies. He brought his hand down with as much force as he could muster, smacking her right across her bum cheeks. Again Tanya whined and wriggled seductively on his lap, her camisole top pulled from her skirt waist, and Frank could see the bare midriff... boy, she was sexy. He swatted her backside with another couple of hard whacks. Left check, right check, a nice steady rhythm. OK, he had spanked the odd prostitute, but punishing a woman for a real misdemeanour was so much more enjoyable - especially a semi-reluctant one like Tanya.

The leather was warming up nicely. Those pert round orbs were nicely moulded to the leather shell of her skirt. Nice and tight. That was how Frank liked it. He raised his hand as high as he could and gripped her grasping wrist, then he gritted his teeth and brought his palm down with an almighty wallop.

"Ouch!" Tanya blasted. Her legs flailed and her blonde mane swept the floor, her large hoop earrings jingling like wind chimes. She released a sob and Frank saw a teardrop fall to the floor. Irresistible. His hand felt sore but he raised it again and again and smashed it into her buttocks. Then he was back to his more rhythmic smacks. She sobbed and moaned and occasionally made a huge wriggling effort to try to escape him. But she was going nowhere. Frank had a very firm hold and he was determined to spank her thoroughly.

He decided to unzip the back of her skirt.

"What the hell are you doing?" she moaned. "You're nothing but a pervert."

"You're the one who had Richardson's cock in your mouth," Frank counter-claimed. The skirt slipped easily down her smooth legs. It reached her ankles and dropped off. The thong could stay, Frank decided; after all it covered virtually no flesh. He raised his hand again and this time brought it down with a splat on Tanya's bare flesh. She released a cry and told him to stop and sobbed and pleaded, but Frank turned a deaf 'un. Instead he built up a relentless rhythm, beating one buttock and then the other on alternate strokes. Smack! Wallop! Splat!

Tanya yelped and wriggled and begged for release, but Frank was enjoying himself for the first time in years. All the women who had rejected him for being too fat, all the women who had taken the piss out of him - he could see their faces on Tanya's reddening buttocks. After he had walloped each in turn for a good ten minutes he finally had to give up. His hand hurt and he was exhausted. Sweat streamed down his face - a Santa costume would certainly not be the dress of choice for any wannabe spanker, he thought.

As he breathed deeply he felt Tanya panting, draped over his knees, and every now and again she released a small sob.

"I thought I could trust you," she moaned.

"And so you can," Frank said. "I've written Richardson a resignation letter because I'm fed up with this 'Santa gig', as he calls it. If you get that letter off Richardson's desk and dispose of it I'll set him up and do us both a favour. I'll make sure he never pesters you again, and I'll ensure I never have to wear a red Santa suit unless I want to."

"I don't believe you."

"It's true."

Slowly, Tanya slipped to her knees. She crouched at his feet.

"I suppose I deserved it," she said. "But that hurt. None of my other boyfriends have ever smacked me that hard. With them it's always been playful."

Frank just loved the idea of being considered a boyfriend.

She stood up and whispered in his ear. "Now I've been properly punished does Santa have any pressies in his sack for me?"

Frank smiled. She was still coming on to him. Maybe the spanking had made her as randy as he was. Her next words confirmed his suspicions.

"Come on, Frankie-boy, you know what to do," she breathed. "I've always fancied getting laid in a grotto by a real live Santa. It's been a fantasy of mine since I was a teenager, and now you've punished me I think it's only right and proper that you pleasure me."

Frank couldn't believe his luck. This was Tanya, the best looking girl in the department store coming on to him! Her hand delved under his Santa hood and rubbed his damp hair.

"What about Richardson?" he asked. "Won't he be looking for you?"

"Richardson won't bother us in here. This is Santa's secret grotto and Richardson's too busy chasing reluctant females at the office party."

Tanya's lips impacted on his like two red missiles. Frank opened his mouth and closed his eyes. He let her tongue whirl around his. This was the best Christmas present he'd ever had. No question.

Tanya loosened his red gown and pulled it open, then she stood back. To combat the warmth of the outfit Frank only wore a pair of boxers under the robe, so once loosened, his boxers were exposed, and without Tanya's bum or tum to repress it his pink-headed cock popped up like a jack in the box.

"My goodness, I've seen some meat in my time, Frankie, but that's got to be the biggest!" Tanya exclaimed.

Frank smiled at the compliment; there were compensations for being a fat slob, and one was a tool in proportion to his body mass index. Big, thick and sturdy, it was a juggernaut amongst cars. It was just a pity that the normal surveyors of its fine form were prostitutes who hung around the train station or the Oriental girls who worked in the massage parlours.

"Show me what you did for Richardson," he demanded, and without a word she bent to her knees as if worshipping the large obelisk. She took it in both hands and placed her scarlet, spongy lips over the tip. Like a true pro her wet mouth eased over his helmet. Soon she was working his shaft up and down, up and down, coating his penis in a thin layer of gloss and sparkle. Frank was in heaven, and moments later his cock erupted.

"You dirty sod, Santa!" Tanya spat, wiping her mouth. "You could have warned me you were about to come!"

"Santa wanted to give you a present," he grinned.

She smiled seductively. "But I want another present. It's time that meat was cooked in the oven. Let's just hope you can rise to the occasion a second time."

Frank knew there would be no fear of that. The thought of having sex with Tanya was worth a lorry load of Viagra.

She slipped out of her thong and sat astride him. Then, like a gymnast on parallel bars, one hand on each thigh, she lowered herself onto his rock-hard organ. Frank felt her sex slowly encase his standing stalk. Inch by blissful inch her wet pussy slid onto his upright, uptight cock. Frank had to keep repeating to himself *I'm fucking Tanya Webb, the best, most horny woman at Jacobs*. It was unbelievable. With a yelp of pleasure she sank down on him until she had engulfed all his thick, fleshy column. Frank's cock pushed up and expanded inside her vagina, impaling her on a spike of pleasure.

"Christ almighty, that thing's pushing up against my stomach!" Tanya exclaimed deliriously. She steadied herself and slowly rode back and forth, back and forth, lifting her thighs to ensure her vagina got the full benefit of Frank's mighty member. He flexed his stomach muscles and pumped his cock up and down in time with her rhythmic grinding. He could feel her warm love juices seeping out around the base of his manhood. His hands smothered her nylon-covered breasts. He held them in his hands, squeezing them gently like stress balls, in time to the rocking rhythm of their bodies. He could feel her lacy bra beneath the top and every now and then his fingers felt her baby-soft flesh.

Tanya bounced up and down as if she were sitting astride a trotting horse. Her flushed and red face was so near to his, Frank could see the mascara on her eyelashes, the kohl around her eyes. It had been a long time since he had been close to a woman as beautiful as Tanya. A long time. He knew he was about to explode but held off and held off. Fighting nature, fighting desire, fighting, fighting, fighting...

Tanya's breathing became more hurried and her movements faster and faster. What was she thinking? *I'm fucking Santa Clause?* Frank gazed into the deep blue depths of her eyes and knew they revealed a passionate secret. Maybe her first sexual encounter had been with a Santa under a Christmas tree at home, or maybe she had lost her virginity to a Santa in a grotto. Frank didn't know but he knew for sure that Tanya had the hots for men in red suits who came once a year.

She grabbed his shoulders and squeezed. "Fuck me, Santa," she whispered, closing her eyes and stretching back her neck. "Fuck me, Santa."

Bracing her nicely warmed buttocks, Frank pushed his cock up into her as hard as he possibly could, ejaculating into her tight passage with such force he slid down on the chair. Tanya was rocked back by the eruption; she grabbed the hairs on his chest to steady herself. Her eyes closed as she too climaxed, her vagina forming a vicelike ring around his cock as her muscles tightened. Tightened, tightened... tightened... then relaxed...

"Oh, Santa, that was so fucking good, so good," she moaned.

Moments later she eased off him. Frank felt his cock deflate. Tanya would never know how desperate he had been for sex. Well, she had certainly done her best to help those in sexual need at Christmas - perhaps it really was the time of year for giving.

"I'd better get to the party," she said wearily. "Richardson will be wondering where I am by now. You not joining us?"

"No, I need to freshen up." Frank knew he looked a mess. "But if you want to get back at Richardson then I've got a plan."

"What is it?" she asked.

"Go back to the party and lead Richardson on. Then, tell him I've gone home and you'd like sex with him in the grotto... leave the rest to me."

"You really think you can get Richardson off my back?"

"I sure can."

"OK, I'll see you in a bit." She ran a hand through her blond hair and straightened her skirt, then folded her mac over her arm. Frank knew that when she left the grotto she would find her way to the bathroom so she could reapply her make-up. Women were good at hiding their indiscretions. After all, they carried the tricks of the trade in their handbags.

"Oh, and remember to get that letter back, and when you do just shred it. I won't be needing to resign as I can guarantee I won't be Santa next year. Though with you around there are certain perks to the job."

"I'll get it," she assured him.

When she had gone Frank went to the public toilet and had a wash and straightened up his own clothes, then he made a few calls to a couple of friends and waited. Tanya sent a text to say she had shredded his letter of resignation, but otherwise all was quiet.

It was nearly nine-thirty when Frank heard the clip-clop of Tanya's heels on the mall floor. He peeked out of the grotto to see her leading Richardson towards the entrance. He had a drink in his hand and looked half cut. Frank quickly moved to a corner of the grotto where he was out of sight.

"Oh, Dennis," Tanya said, in the same seductive voice she had used on him. "Let's do it in here. I've always fantasised about making love in a grotto."

Frank could see Richardson's hands were all over her, mauling her breasts and up her smooth legs. Frank suddenly felt protective of her, but he kept his mobile aimed at the randy couple and kept recording - pictures and sound. These modern bits of kit were wonderful. Certainly Mrs Richardson would get a surprise if her deviant sex-mad husband ever tried it on with Tanya again. When Frank had enough footage he placed the camera back in his pocket. The area where he was hiding was slightly raised behind an artificial boulder, so with Richardson looking down on Tanya there was no way he could be seen, so Frank slowly rose to his full height. He breathed in to expand his chest like Tarzan in the jungle, and then jumped into the air. With an almighty bang he landed on the floor of the grotto beside a bemused Richardson.

"What the hell?" Richardson exclaimed.

"Surprise! Surprise!"

Just at that moment the two elves emerged from their hiding place and took Richardson's clothes. Frank got his mobile out and let the camera roll again.

"What the fuck's going on?" Richardson demanded.

"I won't be asked to play Santa next year will I, Richardson?" Frank asked.

"No," the naked man said, trying to hide his erection. "Now get those two dwarfs to give me back my clothes."

"And you'll stop pestering Tanya for sex, or your wife gets the footage."

"I thought she..." then his head dropped and he realised he'd been set up. He was beaten. "OK," he said. "I won't harass her ever gain... I just need that camera... please don't show my wife..."

"And while we're at it," Frank continued, enjoying himself immensely, "I want the manager's job you've been advertising. I never applied because I thought you wouldn't give me a chance, but now I've caught you with your trousers down the tables have turned."

Richardson nodded. "You're pushing it too far, Frank... But if that's what you want, it's yours."

Frank pocketed his phone for a second time and called back the elves.

As Richardson got dressed he said, "I couldn't help but notice your bum's rather hot, Tanya. Has this man been spanking you?"

Tanya blushed. "Yes, he knows about what I did earlier in the week and thought it was very naughty - even though you made me do it."

Richardson turned to Frank. "That deal we just made about not harassing Tanya? It doesn't apply to punishing errant secretaries, does it?"

"No, no of course not, Mr Richardson," Frank said. "You must do whatever you think fit when it comes to disciplining your staff."

"Frankie, no!" Tanya exclaimed.

"Oh yes, Tanya," Frank said. "And if I'm going to be a manager as well, I might just have to discipline you too."

Richardson smiled at Frank, and the two men shook hands on what appeared to be a highly satisfactory arrangement.

CANING CHANTELLE
The Jilted Boyfriend's Tale

In some ways I still can't believe it happened on Saturday night in the way it did - I just can't believe it. I mean it is just so, so out of character for me to react the way I did, do what I did I mean, because, let's be honest, it was not a reaction - far from it. But, I mean, moi? No way!

It concerns Chantelle, of course, lovely, bubbly, beautiful Chantelle Harris. We met in a nightclub. She was wearing a tight-fitting, strapless black dress - which highlighted her ample bust to perfection. Chantelle was certainly a looker, and she knew it. We had a kiss and a slow dance and we exchanged numbers. The next day I called her and I asked her out on a date. I called in hope more than expectation, but she accepted without telling me she had a boyfriend already. First mistake. Even so, I was a placid chap and, when she ditched him, I was happy. After all, it was hard to believe that a young woman as beautiful as Chantelle would not be always attached. And after Brian, the former beau, had gone Chantelle was mine, all mine.

She lived with her mum in a small semi and worked as a PA in a large company. Mrs Harris - or Diane - was pleasant and I used to chat to her as I waited to collect Chantelle, who always took a long time to get ready when we went out for the night. But it was worth it. When she eventually came downstairs to greet me with a short tight skirt showing her slim legs off to a tee, boy, was she worth it! I loved the looks I got from other men when I took her out. I felt on top of the world. Me, Andy, the loser, had pulled a stunner and was a real dude. It was something I could only dream about. When at school I had been something of a victim, often catching the end of a fist or a kick in the shins. I'd left school and worked in various jobs until a piece of good fortune had arrived at my door in the form of a job in a small business owned by Mr Jobson. Mr Jobson took a shine to me; he had no family of his own and I think I became something of a surrogate son. Anyway, I quickly made progress working for him. We shared a passion for racehorses and sometimes went racing together, and that's where a second piece of luck befell me, because a year before I met Chantelle I won a large bet on the Tote at Cheltenham and netted over £50,000. I was quids in and as happy as Larry. I put the deposit down on a flat and bought a new car. All I needed was the girl and that's where Chantelle kindly obliged.

To be frank, I was aware she was a bit of a gold-digger. On our first date she bragged about the cars her former boys had driven and how much they earned, how much she had spent on a handbag, shoes, a dress, and how rich her boss was, whose name was John and who of course adored her - in Chantelle's eyes everyone adored her. Put simply, in the words of Oscar Wilde, she knew the price of everything and the value of nothing. But is that so different from a lot of people these days?

Our relationship was fairly conventional. We went out of meals and to the cinema and eventually we made love at my flat - after I'd cooked her a meal. She loved the fact she had a boyfriend with a flat and a car, and that we could do adult things like have dinner at my place. She even added her feminine touch to my abode by selecting some of my furnishings.

Also, we went away for weekends. I paid of course - Chantelle expected nothing less - and it was worth it for the green-eyed looks of jealousy I got from other men when I bowled into a restaurant with Chantelle on my arm.

Mr Jobson always said, "It pays to think big, Andy, it pays to think big," and, though I knew he would admonish me if he knew I never expected Chantelle to hang around long with me, those words came to me frequently when I was out with her. For one, brief shining moment I felt successful. I was happy. Happy with my trophy girlfriend. The loser had come good. Andy Collins was a loser no more.

So to my account of events that Saturday night. Three, maybe four weeks before we were in a local pub having a quiet drink - even in her tight jeans and trainers Chantelle looked hot. I took a sip of my pint and she flicked back her blonde hair.

"Look Andy," she said. "I know you're probably planning a surprise for my birthday (I wasn't) but unfortunately I've been asked to go on a course down in Margate and it's the week of my birthday."

"It won't be the whole week, will it?" I asked.

She nodded slowly, simultaneously releasing a thin smile.

"What's the course?" I asked, somewhat surprised.

"John wants me to learn about marketing and sales. He thinks I'm wasted as a PA and wants me to be a bit more ambitious. Why should I let you men take all the best jobs? I plan to strike a blow for feminism."

You could start by going Dutch, I thought, but was too enthralled by my little coquette to utter the words.

"That's good," I said, not really knowing what to say. "It's great that John thinks you're so capable. I'm sure you would be good in sales... and marketing."

"So you don't mind?" Chantelle asked rather coyly.

"Of course not," I said, slightly surprised. "I wouldn't stand in the way of anyone's career, if that's what you want, go for it. 'Think big', as Mr Jobson always says."

"Just do it," she said, repeating a sportswear company's catchphrase and showing she already had a feel for the subject. "I'm so pleased you don't mind."

I assured her again that I didn't and thought no more about it. Although I would miss her a week apart was hardly the end of the world, and my poor old wallet would be given a bit of a rest. Then my brain turned to things that can happen on these residential courses. "No flings," I said. "That's my one stipulation, no flings."

Chantelle giggled, leant over and kissed me on the check.

"Andy, you're so sweet. I really love you. Most of my boyfriends have been really controlling and possessive and never let me do my own thing - you're not like that. You're kind and generous and understanding. You only want what's best for me and I love you for it."

She could have added that I was a mug but that would come later. I thought no more of her little jolly and didn't ask her any more questions. Second mistake.

So Chantelle went off down to Margate. I had wanted to see her go but she said that another woman from work was going and would give her a lift. We went out the night before and I told her that when she got back I would plan a lovely surprise for her at my flat to make up for her missed birthday. Then, on the Monday she was gone. She promised to text rather than phone, claiming that texting was the easiest and simplest way to keep in touch.

I was actually enjoying my week without Chantelle - I certainly had a bit more money in the old sky rocket and was able to shoot the breeze with one or two friends. One lunchtime I was minding my own, walking down the High Street, when I ran in to Sue, a friend of Chantelle's. I said hello but she ignored me, so I walked up to her.

"Hi Sue."

"Hi Andy."

"Heard from Chantelle?" I asked.

"The odd text... what about you?"

"The same, we agreed not to phone."

"I suppose it's difficult," Sue said.

"With all those delegates, sure, but we have had the odd convo," I said.

"Delegates?"

"Yes, on her training course."

"Training course?"

"Yes, in Margate."

"Margate?"

"Yes, bloody Margate."

"I thought she was in..." Sue stopped. She looked at me, she went crimson, she put her hand to her mouth. "Oh my God, you don't know, do you? Oh my God, she hasn't told you yet, has she? Oh Andy, I'm so sorry... me and my big mouth... I've really put my foot in it... I'm so sorry!"

And with that she disappeared.

When it comes to women I'm probably not the sharpest at picking up clues, which is why I've been taken for a ride more times than a rollercoaster at Thorpe Park, but it was quite clear that Chantelle's Margate trip was a porky pie. As I say, I have always got on well with Diane, her mother, so that night I decided to pay her a visit. I followed her through to the front room and explained my chat with Sue.

"Do you know what's going on, Diane?" I asked.

She made me a cup of tea and sat down. "It's very naughty of Chantelle not to tell you, but unfortunately, Andy, she's found another boyfriend called Clive and she's going to ditch you when she gets back from holiday."

"Where is she now then?"

"Clive's taken her to Sharm-el-Sheikh for her birthday."

I couldn't believe it. I stared down at the carpet, tears in my eyes. I knew Chantelle was not for life, but I had expected a bit more than a few months before I was dumped.

"Why didn't she tell me before she went?" I asked naively. But I already knew the answer; the little gold-digger wanted to max out on birthday presents. She wanted to take the presents from me and maybe give me the old tin tack the following week. I knew Chantelle well enough to know that. Her mum confirmed it.

"I suspect she wanted to see what you'd bought for her birthday. She always said you were the most generous of her boyfriends."

Diane came over to me and sat on the arm of the chair. She rubbed my shoulder. "I wish she wouldn't do this. I wish she would play fair by her boyfriends. God knows where she gets it from, I was never like her."

"I know, Diane," I said. "I wish she was more like you."

I clenched and unclenched my fist to pump the poison of a love betrayed out of my system. I felt angry. Bloody angry.

Diane slipped off the arm of the chair and with sudden aggression said, "I'm not proud to call Chantelle my daughter the way she's behaved towards you. That girl needs her arse tanned, she really does."

Mr Jobson was of the same opinion when I cornered him at work and told him my tale of woe.

"Andy," he said, "it may not be politically correct but in my day a minx like that would have been punished. Soundly."

That got my mind working. I was a placid guy not given to aggression or over-emotional responses. I was normally pretty calm and collected and had never hit anyone in my life - even though the bullies had picked on me at school. But if she was going to ditch me anyway what was wrong with going out with a bang?

I checked out her Facebook page. Maybe that was something I should have done from the start to keep tabs on the little cheat. It was quite easy to see that Chantelle was a party girl who liked male attention. There were numerous photos of her with her arms draped around men smoking and drinking and giggling - some since she had met me. It made sense - those girls' nights out had probably ended with a guy taking her back to his place and all the while I had played the dutiful boyfriend. And now this: Sharm-el-Sheikh with Clive of bloody Indian or wherever - while she told me she was on a course in Margate.

As the week went on I kept up the pretence of not knowing. I enjoyed texting Chantelle and asking her about her course. We even spoke a couple of times on the phone; no doubt Clive was down by the pool. And, with Mr Jobson's able and very knowledgeable assistance I started planning my revenge.

I started sowing the seeds with texts to Chantelle to say I had bought her some presents and that was all my Cheltenham winnings gone.

I texted to say I could not wait to see her again and I had booked a lovely Italian restaurant; Chantelle loved pizza. She texted back to say she was missing me and couldn't wait to come home and see me and celebrate her birthday with me. She texted *the course is sooooooo boring. YAWN!* My, what a little actress she was! Still, I was ready for her. Ready and waiting.

She arrived home on Friday evening and I arranged to see her on Saturday night. I'd spoken to Diane again and asked her not to say anything about our conversation as I wanted Chantelle to tell me in person and give me her reasons for dumping me. Diane was more than happy with this arrangement; clearly she did not want to get involved and who could blame her.

So to the Saturday. I collected Chantelle that evening as normal; she was wearing a lovely red dress which was nice and short and showed off her tanned bare legs to perfection. Amazing how much sun there is in Margate! Her heels must have been a good five inches and when she slithered into my car and gave me a kiss on the cheek with those glossy red lips and told me how much she had missed me I almost lost my resolve and was tempted to forgive her on the spot. God, she was hot! My joy stick, which had only had Madam Palm and her five lovely daughters for company all week, was already feeling hard!

I drove slowly back to my flat, talking idly and asking about her trip to Margate. It was fun listening to her lies.

"There was this one girl called Sally," she said. "She just would not shut up and whenever the tutor asked the question she piped up all the time. Right foghorn, she was, spoilt it for everyone else."

It was amazing to hear her and, had I not known differently, I would have been sucked in to her lies and delusions.

We arrived home and I insisted on a walk up the stairs to my fourth floor apartment. I wanted to take it easy, to gather my thoughts and also, in my jacket pocket I had a blindfold and knew that as soon as I put it on her there was no going back. We reached my door.

"Wait," I said gently. "Inside is your birthday present. I want it to be a surprise. I want you to wear a blindfold until you're in the flat."

Chantelle beamed. Her eyes sparkled with avaricious contentment. This was what she had wanted, why she would not dump me before the trip to Sharm-el-Sheik with Clive.

I took the thick black eye bind from my pocket. She dutifully turned around like a ballerina on a music box and allowed me to secure it into place. I swept my hand in front of her face as a magician might do to check she really could not see anything. Then I unlocked my front door. Taking her by the arm I led her down the short hall, into the front room. She was taking small steps in her high heels and placing her hands in front of her to feel for obstructions.

"Don't worry, I've got you," I said.

Her dress rustled as she moved. She was slightly bent down, scared of falling, her sight removed from her senses. I had left music playing, only softly, but I wanted music on. George Gershwin. Chantelle didn't like classic music but who cared? This was not about her, this was about me. When the time arrived I would turn it up with the remote and fast forward, to "Walking the Dog" - it was an appropriate track.

I led her into the centre of the room and made her stand up straight with her hands at her sides. She was so anxious to get the present she was still smiling, her heart pumping beneath the tight bodice of the dress, pumping with excitement, anticipation. I had an erection just looking at her. Vulnerable. Clueless. Defenceless. Totally oblivious to what was in front of her. I knew I had to be careful. I knew the operation had to be delicately handled so as not to arouse suspicion.

"Chantelle, I'm going to gently move you forward. I will lean you forward, but don't be scared; you're not going to fall."

"Why? Where's the present?"

"The presents," I said, emplacing the plural, "are on the floor in front of you. I want you to touch them before you see them."

I placed a hand on her toned stomach and one on her back. I leant her forward, very slowly, her feet not moving. Eventually she was resting against the thick padding of the whipping horse. A quick push and she was over it. She released a little yelp but before she could do anything I snapped cuffs to her wrists to bind her to the horse. Then I pushed her legs apart as the police might do and snapped restraints to her ankles.

"What the hell's going on, Andy?" she squealed. "Release me!"

My heart was beating so hard I really thought I might have a heart attack, my hands sweaty, but I had Chantelle where I wanted her - over the whipping horse. My cock was bursting from my trousers. I had never felt so erotically charged. Mr Jobson had warned me not to let the erotic get in the way of the punishment, but it was difficult. I took a sip of whiskey. I had left the glass sitting on the mantelpiece ready to calm my nerves, next to the stereo remote. I turned up the volume and fast-forwarded to "Walking the Dog". Gentle, melodic music. I took another sip of whiskey and untied Chandelle's blindfold; I wanted to see the blue of her eyes and I wanted her to see me.

The smile had gone and replaced with a scowl.

"What are you doing, Andy? This isn't funny, this is scary. Release me!"

"Don't you want your present?"

"Where is it?" she asked.

I smiled; even in such a compromising position she could not believe that I had not bought her a present!

I walked over to the TV and picked up a long thin item wrapped in birthday paper.

"It's here, Chantelle, its here."

"What the fuck is it?"

"I'll unwrap it for you, as you're incapacitated."

My hands sweated. I was so nervous I had a job pulling the paper off. It wasn't hard to work out what the long thin object with the crooked handle was. Not hard at all.

"Oh no..." Chantelle said. "I'm not having that."

"But it's your birthday present," I said.

"You're mad, Andy. Now release me!"

I waved the cane through the air to make a swishing sound. I felt powerful. Invincible.

"But why, Andy? Why have you turned so psycho on me?"

I was waiting for this. Waiting for the question. I knew exactly what I was going to say. I wasn't going to accuse her of anything or make accusations or ask who the hell

Clive was and how she had met him. Those things were incidental. There was just one word - well three actually - and they said all I needed to say.

I whisked the cane through the air again and as I did so I said, "Sharm-el-Sheikh." I had never been there but knew it was in Egypt and a popular tourist destination.

"Who told you?" she asked.

I wasn't speaking.

"All right, I shouldn't have gone. I should have told him 'no'. I love you, Andy. You're the one. If I learnt nothing else there it was that."

I didn't speak.

"Please, Andy, give me one more chance. I'll never cheat on you again as long as I live, and you can have other women if you wish. I don't mind."

I wasn't speaking.

She tried another tack. "Didn't you realise we were both just friends with benefits and we could play around? I thought I'd made that clear."

I still did not talk. No, while she was talking I pulled down her lovely silky knickers and pushed up her satin dress. Her pert bottom was exposed. Her buttocks twitched. She tried one last time.

"I'll scream. I'll call the police."

I laughed. I walked to the chair and picked up some duct tape. It was silver and didn't match her dress, but no one else was going to see her. A strip of it was soon covering her mouth. She hissed and huffed. And those lovely eyes glistened with tears - with hate. I walked back to the cane and whistled it through the air. Once. Twice. Three times.

Each time she flinched and her buttocks tensed. The feeling of power was unbelievable. I raised my cane - correction, Chandelle's cane, as it was my present to her - high in the air. Then with all the force I could muster I slashed it down across her buttocks with a sharp swipe.

Chantelle jerked against the horse as if she'd received an electric shock. She winced and let out a muffled yelp.

"No, no, no," she mumbled through her gag.

"Sharm-el-Sheik," I repeated.

Again the cane rippled through the air, this time leaving a thin red line across both her buttocks, though it was more prominent on her right cheek. I evened things up with the next stroke. Mr Jobson had told me that the art of caning was even strokes close to or on top of existing ones. All week I had practiced using a marker pen and a pillow. Now for the real deal. I raised my arm again and brought the cane down, jumping in the air as I did so to maximise the impact. The cane whistled through the air before whipping into Chantelle's buttocks. She released another muffled yelp as the impact jolted her forward. She was trying to tell me to stop. Tears dripped from her eyes onto my carpet. I was far from finished. I raised the cane again and brought it down on her arse with a thunderous crack. The thin red mark was growing wider and redder. She writhed on the horse and tried to free herself from the bindings, trying in vain to get off the horse and remove her bum from the awful pain. And still Gershwin played. I stood back and looked at my handiwork. My cock was fit for bursting out of my trousers. I raised the cane again and again jumped in the air to maximise impact. The cane walloped into her backside and rocked the whole horse forward. Chantelle really was crying now. Big blobs of tears fell onto the carpet. The duct tape muffled her screams and counterpointed neatly with Gershwin's 'dog walking'. The next stroke was across the back of her legs and made her gasp. It was as unexpected as it was painful. I gave her another couple of strokes on the back of her legs - two thin red lines appeared on both her thighs. It was nice work. Then back to the buttocks for another three hard as hell strokes that made her wail like a baby through the reliable tape. God, I was turned on!

When finished I took off my shirt and trousers and stood behind her ravaged buttocks in my underpants. I had bought some baby lotion and started to work it into her arse. I knew it would be soothing. I rubbed it in and added the odd slap for good measure. Her buttocks were awesome: lovely rounded globes, white and ripe and firm. I loved kneading them when we made love, but kneading them when they had been well and truly thrashed, well that surpassed all expectations. I traced the red wheals with my fingers: I let my fingers travel up her crack to find a deliciously wet clit. Despite the pain she had obviously enjoyed the thrashing.

I finally released my eager cock from my pants. I pulled them off and was completely naked. I removed the gag from her mouth. I expected a stream of abuse from her. Her make-up had run and her chest heaved. I could see she was unable to understand the assault that had just taken place. She looked at my erection with those glorious blue eyes, silently questioning why a nice guy had turned so wild. I suspect she knew what was going to happen; she didn't have to be an Einstein to work out what I was going to do next. I moved back behind her, close so I could feel the heat of her buttocks against my groin. Then I felt her sex again, wet and hot and inviting. I pushed my cock up and in, fucking her doggy-style for all I was worth. The horse rocked back and forth, back and forth as I pushed my cock deep into her.

"Oh my God... oh my God... oh my God..." she mumbled repeatedly.

I had never experienced anything like it, and very soon my cock exploded inside her, and her cunt tightened around my trunk as she too convulsed in orgasm.

I withdrew my dripping member and wiped a tissue over the head, then still leaving her tied up I quickly got dressed, then released her from her bonds. She was speechless. Completely silent. She just did not know what to do. She pulled down her satin dress and tried to smarten herself up, but her eyes were still blotchy and her hair was a mess.

"Come on," I said.

"Where are we going?"

"Home."

I led her out of my flat by the arm and down to my car. I drove her home.

"Chantelle, whatever's happened to you?" Diane gasped.

That was when the floodgates opened. "Mum, he caned me!" Chantelle fell into her mother's arms, but the look on Diane's face was something to behold; a mixture of bewilderment and wonderment.

"I'll be off then, Mrs Harris," I said. "It's been nice knowing you and dating your daughter. I trust you'll get on well with Clive, and that they'll live happily ever after. Please tell Chantelle to put tonight's little episode down to experience and we'll say no more about it."

As I spoke I edged down the drive. I wanted away. I got into my car and sped off. For all the confidence and bravado I was scared stiff that the police would be called and I'd be arrested for assault. Fortunately Mr Jobson had promised me that if

66

anything did go wrong I would keep my job, and as soon as I got back to my flat I phoned him and replayed the details. In fact, he asked me to phone him back so he could make himself more comfortable. Then I started to talk, to tell him the story of Chantelle's caning, and he kept stopping me and asking me to repeat bits. He kept saying, "Detail, Andy, detail."

I was on the phone for over an hour that night, and when I went to work on Monday my first job was to write an account of the events that led to the caning of Chantelle, which is what you have here. He said it would help if I wrote down the facts while the events were fresh in my mind, just in case the police were called. I spent the whole day writing this report, which I emailed to Mr Jobson at the end of the day. He emailed back with a cryptic message that read *Sex is sadism and love is masochism.*

I didn't really understand what he meant until later that evening, for when I got home there was a bunch of flowers and a box of chocolates standing outside my door. At first I thought they had gone to the wrong address; surely they were for a woman?

I looked at the card. The message attached to the flowers read: *Andy, thank you for the best birthday present ever... ever. I know I deserved it. Do you forgive me? Please, please call. Love you, C XXX.*

I unlocked my front door and took the flowers and chocolates inside and placed them on the table. So Chantelle really was a glutton for punishment, was she? Maybe that was her last mistake. And mine.

PADDLING PANDORA

The Personal Assistant's Tale

I could see them now from where I was lurking under the desk. It wasn't how I had planned it. How I had imagined it. Not at all. I was expecting to have more time and when the theatre ended I had intended to relocate to a cupboard in Fraser's office, which had a convenient keyhole. Now I was taken unawareness and I knew I would need a slice of good luck to see the action... if there was to be any action. The voices were getting louder. Approaching...

I've always liked my job, that is jobs - plural, as I have worked as a PA for a number of different companies and I'm very good at it. That's my job - being a PA, or a Personal Assistant, if you prefer. I was born in Newark, New Jersey and I'm fairly slim with brown curly hair and large glasses; I like the secretarial look. I'm of average build and I always dress well. Not necessarily fashionable but, well... oh, and I'm thirty-five years of age, unattached and live in an apartment on the outskirts of London.

But back to my job. I'm well-organised and I love sorting out the men in my life, whether it's my boyfriends or my bosses. In many ways a PA has control. She - and it usually is a she - holds the diary and makes appointments. She also acts as a gatekeeper to those who want to see the top guy. Oh yes, I'm good at my job and have not been for an interview for years, as on the last three occasions I've been headhunted and earned more money working for more powerful bosses. In fact, ever since I came over to England twelve years ago with my then employer, I've been headhunted, so that shows you how darn good I am. And let me tell you straight, the more powerful my boss is the more I enjoy my job. Period. Describe myself in three words? Smart, sassy, bossy - that's me.

The most powerful person I've worked for was Mr D. J. Starchier. Mr Starchier ran his own business, was a self-made millionaire and ran a company employing over a thousand people. When his PA left to start a family he hired me. He knew me from a colleague and he took me out to dinner and put an offer on the table. An offer I could not refuse. I knew he would be a good boss to work for as he spoke about his old PA in gushing terms, and I knew straightaway that she had been a big part of his life. He was just the type who would want to have his home life organised as well as his work life, which was just how I liked it.

He was eighteen years older than me and he was not at all good-looking in the conventional sense, but he had a certain charm and charisma which made him a pleasure to work for. And he was powerful - always an aphrodisiac.

I think I'd been in post for about a year when he told me he had forgotten his wife's birthday and asked me to pop out and buy a card, which I did. His wife, I should say, was a dusky South American beauty. She was in her early thirties and had lovely dark, shoulder-length hair, a figure to die for and she always dressed to the nines. They had two children - a boy and a girl - and Mrs Starchier was a full-time mum. Only of course she wasn't at all as she had a cleaner, a cook, a nanny and a gardener, so poor Mrs Starchier had nothing to do all day bar go shopping, look after her figure in the gym, lunch with friends and visit endless beauty parlours. Oh, and ride her horse. She was, in short, a trophy wife - spelt with a capital "T".

She came into the office on a few occasions and I summed her up instantly as a bimbo who hung on to the arm of an indulgent husband but had never done a day's work in her life. I could see she loved nothing more than flaunting her designer clothes and her gold jewellery. Not a hair on her head was out of place and her make-up was immaculate. She always pouted with those shiny lips of hers; she certainly was one hot babe and no mistake.

So I bought a card, nothing strange about that. I had done it before for bosses. And me being me I put a note in my secret personal diary, the one I kept records in about all my bosses. 8th November was Pandora's birthday. That info was transferred to my home PC with a little memory flag which meant the following year I could remind Mr Starchier.

"Fraser, it's your wife's birthday next week, have you got her something nice?" The secret of the successful PA is the subtle reminder; you don't want the poor man to look stupid.

"God, yea, you're right Madison, I'd forgotten clean about it," Mr Starchier sighed.

"Do you want me to get a card?" I volunteered, ever helpful.

"You couldn't do the honours, could you?" he asked.

He went to his wallet and thumbed through some notes.

"That's a lot for a card," I said, looking at least ten twenty-pound notes.

"You couldn't get a present as well, could you?"

"What shall I get?"

"Perfume. I don't know."

Fortunately, I knew what perfume she wore as I had smelt it on her when she came to the office one time - and duly noted it in my personal diary. So I bought her a bottle of that and a card. I wrapped it up neatly for Fraser and left it on his desk.

"She loved it," he said later. "She was very impressed I knew what perfume she wore. You're a genius, Madison."

A few months later and 14th Feb was approaching so, in the same subtle manner, I asked if he had bought her anything. Of course he hadn't and I was tasked with buying a card. But this time I was a little bit cheeky.

"What about some sensual lingerie?" I suggested.

Fraser smiled. I could see he was tempted. He knew it was something he should be buying but he knew my choices would be so much better than his. Of course, there was the issue of Pandora's sizes.

"She looks a size ten or twelve to me," I said.

"Yes, I think she is a size ten," Fraser agreed, but I could tell he didn't have a clue. Breasts were easy. It transpired that Fraser had paid for her to have them enhanced and knew they were a 38B.

That lunchtime I made a visit to an exclusive store and bought some lingerie. Apparently Pandora was again impressed. From then on Fraser didn't need to ask me, he would just unfold some notes and I would go forth and buy lingerie, perfume and jewellery to spice up their relationship or for a special occasion. I suggested he buy Pandora some flowers or a present out of the blue, from time to time, which of course I chose. Everything was carefully noted in my diary and transferred to my computer when I was home. It was amazing how I was building up a picture of Fraser and his wife.

One day he came into work and said, "She thinks I'm having an affair; my presents have never been so good."

I don't know why I enjoyed it so much but I did. And when Pandora walked into the office one day to see Fraser I couldn't help but wonder if she was wearing a pair of knickers and/or a bra I had purchased. I must admit I found a sadistic enjoyment in the idea that she was happily wearing clothes I'd chosen, thinking they were loving gifts selected by a devoted husband, not by a man in a hurry who had no time for such trivia.

That Christmas I bought Pandora a lovely white silky blouse as well as lingerie, a card, jewellery and perfume. It came to over a thousand pounds but Fraser paid, then once wrapped he wrote the tags and then all he had to do was remember what parcel contained what.

"You're the best PA I've ever had, Madison," he said as he kissed me goodnight on Christmas Eve. He opened his wallet and gave me five hundred pounds in cash as a Christmas box, and then he went home to his wife and children, and I went back to my lonely apartment and spent yet another Christmas on my own. I hate that winter break; I've always loathed not being at work.

I never told anyone about the little extras I did for Fraser. Well, I had done them for all my bosses, but more so for Fraser. My motto has always been no job too big, or too small, and that's why I'm the perfect PA, right?

When Fraser came back after Christmas he said Pandora had been suspicious because the parcels were wrapped so well, and questioned him about an affair, until he explained that he'd started to get his presents wrapped professionally, and she'd been appeased.

"Is Pandora on Facebook?" I asked one day.

"Hell, no," Fraser said.

That ruled out one of my sources of information, but I gleaned another. Fraser was very much in control. It came across in the telltale things he would say, and sometimes she would phone him and ask permission to do something or other. He treated her like a child. He was very much the indulgent father and she the spoilt little daddy's girl.

One day he even confessed to me that they'd had a bit of a tiff. He obviously wanted a woman's opinion on whether he had been unfair. Apparently there had been a dinner party, Pandora flirted outrageously and he told her off. She got annoyed and started to cry and said some unpleasant things. I told Fraser he was quite right to act in the way he had, in fact he had probably been too kind to her.

"How do you mean?" he asked.

"Well, it's not my place to say anything, and I don't like to interfere..." even though that was exactly what I was about to do, "but many men might have used a little physical chastisement. A slap, perhaps..."

I left the words hanging. Fraser looked curious. His deep dark eyes peered into me.

"Do people still do that sort of thing?" he asked.

"Oh yes, there's even a name for it - domestic discipline."

"Sounds more like domestic violence to me. I don't want the police knocking on my door."

"They'll only knock if Pandora calls them and it sounds to me, from what you've said, that your Pandora might appreciate a little bit of Alpha male dominance."

Fraser laughed. "God, I pity you if the feminists ever get hold of you. I thought all men were supposed to be feminised wimps who shared their trousers with their women," he joked.

"Is Pandora a feminist?" I probed.

"No, I guess we're more traditional."

"I rest my case."

And I did. I left it standing. The thing is to leave thoughts in people's heads, let them marinate, let Fraser think maybe he had been too soft on Pandora, that she didn't appreciate him. I added that one in during a further conversation, and later added that she took him for granted.

Gradually Fraser was getting the message. Pandora was having a great time going down the gym, having French pedicures and meeting up with her sisterhood of ladies who lunched after a hard day's shopping while he was working his socks off and bankrolling her extravagant lifestyle.

"Yea, when you say it like that..." he mused pensively. "It does seem as if she has the easier deal."

Patience is the key. I didn't rush things. I took it slowly. I loved it when Pandora came into the building; she would walk to Fraser's office and I got to observe her firm, well-toned, gym-tightened bum as she sashayed seductively along the corridor. I just loved watching that bum sway into Fraser's office. I no longer thought about the lingerie she was wearing and whether I had purchased it. No, now I was thinking *you're going to get your lovely bottom smacked, young lady*, and I would feel so turned on, so wet down below, I often had to finger myself in the toilet afterwards. Of course, when Pandora had gone, for I never missed an opportunity to watch her saunter, in her high heels, back through the office and out to the lift. She carried herself with poise and elegance... if not a tad of wealth-inspired arrogance to boot.

"Was she a model?" I asked Fraser one day.

He smiled. "How did you guess? But believe it or not she was too petit and shapely for the catwalk. No, her modelling was lingerie and catalogues. But she's never stuck at anything for long."

"Except for you."

Again his eyes probed into me. "Let's hope so."

"Oh, I'm sure she will never leave you... not once she's received a little training," I teased.

The leather paddle was his next gift to her. Of course, he didn't know it at the time. It was her birthday again so I was sent out to buy, buy, buy. I bought clothes, a card, jewellery and lingerie... and of course, the paddle. I placed it in the box with the lingerie so it would fall out when she picked up the silky camisole top I'd bought her. Once again I wrapped the presents and left them on Fraser's desk. All he had to do was write the tags, and with an almost physic insight he wrote on the lingerie/paddle tag, *Pandora, this is to keep one of us warm! Love, Fraser.*

It was sod's law, as the English say, that her birthday was a weekend and I had to wait until Monday before I saw Fraser again. I just couldn't wait. Unfortunately, first thing he had a meeting and I didn't see him until lunchtime. All the time I kept worrying that maybe I had overstepped the mark - gone too far. So when he arrived at the office I pretended to be deeply involved in my work.

"Madison, can I see you a minute?" he said seriously.

I scuttled behind him into his office. He closed the door.

"What was the meaning of the paddle in my wife's lingerie box?" he said without preamble.

How could I tell him that I dreamed of Pandora being spanked, of her over his knee, over the office desk?

"I think you are too soft with her, Fraser, I think she needs..."

"...A spanking," he concluded. "She said if I ever used that thing on her she'd be suing me for divorce. Of course, I had to make out that I'd bought it, that it was my idea. At least it gave me the chance to open up and tell her I thought she was a spoilt brat, which wasn't the birthday present she'd been expecting."

My sex felt so damp it was untrue. I crossed my legs tightly. "I'm sorry," I said. "I didn't mean to cause any marital strife; I'm just trying to help you, Fraser." I leant across the desk and touched his arm.

He looked circumspect. "I know you are, and I know you're right, I need to put my foot down with Pandora, show her who is boss."

I just loved it - loved that feeling of a masterful Fraser telling Pandora who was in charge. That night I lay in bed and masturbated myself to sleep thinking of that glorious arse being tanned. Little by little I had led Fraser down the path of redemption, shown him another way, as only a woman can.

Each day I hoped he would come to work and tell me he had finally spanked Pandora, but it just didn't happen. He seemed unable or unwilling to perform the task. One day I asked him if the paddle had been used.

"I don't like using it in the house with the kids and staff about."

"What about here?" I ventured, realising that at least he had thought about it.

"That's a possibility," he concurred.

To emphasise the point I bought him another paddle - for office use.

"You're a kinky one and no mistake," he said. "If I didn't know you better I'd think you got turned on by the thought of me punishing my wife."

"I'm just looking after your interests," I said. And I was too. It just so happened, like a lot of men, Fraser did not know what his best interests were.

Once the second paddle had found its way safely to his desk drawer I just had to bide my time. And it was about a month later that he asked me to book a London show for them. It was the usual PA duty which I performed without a hitch. Then, closer to the time, I lifted Pandora's mobile number from his mobile phone. I'd done it before but I wanted to be sure she had not changed numbers. Oh, it was easy enough; he often left his jacket on the chair and his phone and keys on the desk, and of course with the phone I had an opportunity to regularly check messages from and to Pandora. Hence I knew that flirting was a regular theme in their marriage; Pandora flirting with other men and Fraser being annoyed.

Of course, it had been obvious to me for some time that he was concerned that his gorgeous wife may be losing interest in him. From Pandora's viewpoint, marriage to Fraser had opened up a veritable Pandora's Box - excuse the pun - of rich men who liked to be associated with attractive women. Some were married, some were single but all were flirtatious and not surprisingly Pandora responded in kind. This, I had discovered, was one of the reasons why he was so keen on my present choices - bar the paddles; he was scared of losing Pandora and wanted to impress her. So to the theatre.

It was all booked up so I simply had to prepare for the evening. Subtly, I asked Fraser if he was going to meet her in a bar. He said he'd not thought about it so I suggested a bar near the theatre. Next, I engaged the services of a friend of mine who was quite a womaniser. Duncan had bedded countless women and liked nothing more than a bit of seduction. I told him that if he went to the All Inn bar on Thursday night he would meet a ravishing beauty who happened to be married but was "available". He would recognise her, I assured him of that, but to make sure I showed him a picture I had uplifted off Fraser's mobile.

"You're right, she is a babe," Duncan had said, and I knew my plot was in safe hands.

"You know what you have to do?" I asked.

"Yep, when hubby turns up, front up to him and then plague Pandora with salacious texts for the rest of the evening."

"You've got it."

There was nothing more for me to do, the trap was set. I told Fraser I was working late and he went off to the All Inn bar to meet Pandora. In the office block there were companies who worked all through the night, which meant I did not have to check out or tell the security so, instead, I sat watching a movie on my PC - whilst enacting a thousand possible scenarios in my head.

We were ten floors up, the blinds were open and the London skyline sparkled. The light flashed on top of Canary Wharf, the moonlight lit the office. Suddenly I was shocked out of my reverie, surprised to hear the lift whirling and then footsteps, fast footsteps, footsteps along the corridor. I ducked down behind my desk, and then I could hear Fraser's angry voice.

"If I've told you once about flirting, Pandora, I've told you a dozen times!" he shouted.

"But I have no idea where he got my number. I never give it. Honest Fraser. I never once cheat or give it out. Honest to God. Please believe me."

I looked at my watch; they hadn't even made it to the theatre. I had been expecting a long, late night but Fraser clearly had other ideas.

"Where else would that son of a bitch get your fucking number, directory enquiries? Give me a break Pandora. You're nothing but a spoilt little brat who loves taking my money and then cheats on me behind my back."

"Honest, Fraser, I never once did the cheat. Honest Fraser I'm a good Catholic girl. I never do once the cheat. Never. I flirt. Okay, I admit I do the flirt but never I do the cheat. I swear on my Mother's life, God bless her, I never do the cheat."

I could see them now. He had hold of her by the arm. She was wearing the white blouse I had bought her one Christmas and a black leather knee-length skirt. She carried her bag and black coat in her hand. He was marching her to his office. I crouched down further behind the desk. My heart was beating like a drum. What would I say if they saw me? But I was excited and unable to take in what I was watching. Fraser was finally going to punish her! He was finally going to beat the living daylights out of Pandora's sexy arse! Her face was wracked by the anguished annoyance of an innocent. She didn't know yet, but I did. I knew very well what was going to happen next.

Fraser frog-marched her into his office. Thank God he left the door open. I suppose there was no reason to close it, which meant I could come out of my hiding place and position myself by the open door.

"You bitch!" he yelled.

Pandora started crying, sobbing, yelling. "Fraser, I never did the cheat, I never did the cheat!"

But it was too late, all his anxiety about being married to a beautiful South American girl years younger than him came bubbling to the surface in a boiling rage. He released his wife and went to the drawer on the left side of his desk. She was convulsed in sobs. Fraser was back, jacket off, sleeves roughly rolled up. The coat and clutch bag slipped out of her hand to the floor.

"Fraser, believe me, it's true," she begged.

I could feel juices flooding my quim. I had never before seen anything so erotic. God, I longed to finger myself, work myself up. My spine tingled, and mixed with the anxiety of being caught, created a heady mix of ecstasy.

Fraser was in front of Pandora, watching her. A muscle in his cheek pulsed, his face red with rage. He stuffed the paddle into his back pocket, and then grabbed her again by the arm and flung her over the desk. Fortunately it was big and wide and sturdy, as befitted such a powerful man. Pandora went right over it. Her feet kicked out. Moonlight reflected off the shiny black leather of her skirt as her ankles crossed and uncrossed seductively.

"But what are you going to do?" she pleaded.

"Spank you," he said. Even the words sent a shiver through my spine; they were just so erotic, so exciting, so exhilarating.

He took the paddle from his pocket. His free hand pinned Pandora on the desk. He screwed up her white blouse as he pressed her firmly to the desktop. The beautiful leather paddle that I had purchased with my own cash to aid Fraser's matrimonial difficulties was raised high in the air, casting a shadow across the office carpet. The light still flashed on top of Canary Wharf, the moonlight glistened on the Thames - all very twenty-first century, yet somewhere in an air-conditioned office someone was just about to receive a nineteenth century punishment.

The paddle swooped down with a thunderous *thwack*. It splattered onto Pandora's backside. She was shunted forward into the desk, releasing an anguished shriek. But no one could hear her ten floors up, and the one who did hear was enjoying the spectacle too much. Again the leather skirt scrunched as the leather paddle impacted. Pandora shrieked again, and this time Fraser lifted her up by the blouse and thumped her back on the desk.

"Shut up!" he shouted.

The third smack cut both buttocks and must have really hurt as she yelled louder still. Then Fraser was away. The whacks were fast and furious and rained down on her buttocks with an intensity I could only imagine. Poor Pandora, I almost thought. Fraser certainly was mad and when he was mad he was wild.

At last he dropped the paddle to the floor - Pandora's ordeal was over. She sobbed gently, every now and again releasing a violent curse, complaining about him and how she would divorce him and call the police and go back to Peru and he would rot in jail. Sometimes she spoke English, sometimes Spanish.

But he wasn't listening. Instead he unzipped her leather skirt. She was wearing patterned black tights. He manoeuvred himself behind her, and the next thing I saw was the skirt on the floor and her tights and knickers around her ankles. Red blotches appeared on her backside.

"I don't think you could feel anything through the leather," he said. "I think I need to start again."

"But I did, Fraser, I did," she rambled. "It hurt so much I'm crying. I really am crying."

He collected the paddle from the floor and raised it again. Now my love juices really did seep. Fraser beat one buttock and then the other - left, right, left, right, like an army on the march, each buttock receiving an awful beating. Now Pandora was sobbing with the pain, her legs kicked out and he had to stand to one side to avoid them. He smacked, spanked and walloped her that night. To say she received a thoroughly good hiding would be an understatement. She cried and squealed and threatened, but finally all her words were washed away in a sea of sobs.

At last he threw the paddle to the floor. Then he undid his trousers and released his magnificent cock - large and solid and threatening. While she clung to the desk edge he manoeuvred himself into position and pushed his cock into her doggy-style, and I watched in wonderment as he shafted her from behind, sinking his cock into her and fucking her for all he was worth. Finally both man and wife came in unison.

But he was not finished, and with her buttocks as red and rosy and radiant as a blushing bride's face, he pulled her to her feet and gave her a good shake.

"Now don't you ever flirt again, do you hear?" he growled.

"Oh, Fraser, I love you, please believe I never cheat on you!"

And that's when I decided to walk in.

Fraser was surprised, of course. And so was Pandora. I explained to them both that I had set her up with my womanising friend Duncan as I had wanted to teach her a lesson: that flirting can have unintentional consequences. Pandora had all sorts of names for me at that time, starting with "bitch" and escalating, but they are still happily married and Pandora resists the urge to cheat or even flirt. That doesn't mean she doesn't get that superb South American arse of hers thrashed from time to time if she misbehaves in other ways. Since the paddle days Fraser has invested in a number of instruments of punishment: canes, slippers, belts... he even ties her up and gags her.

It's great when he turns to me and tells me he's had to punish her again. I love to hear him relate stories of chastising her. We're usually lying in bed together when he discloses her misdemeanours and his punishments, as he knows how horny I get. And as he does so he fingers or fucks me to a climax. Well, it was inevitable, after all I'd done for him, that we would become lovers.

BELTING BROOKLYN
The Girlfriend's Tale

Steve. What can I say? I met him in a wine bar. I was having a drink with my best friend Claire. We were both singletons having split from boyfriends - hers had been long term, mine short. Well, they all were until I met Steve. Steve was at the bar with some friends, necking bottled beer. He wasn't handsome but he was tall and had tight curly hair. I wouldn't have looked at him twice in the street... in the nightclub... in the pub.

He looked at me though. It started with sidelong glances and then it was stares. Those blue eyes of his peered into me. Read my thoughts. Spied my inner soul. Those unblinking stares. I'm used to men looking. Well, why not? I'm attractive. I have long dark hair and a slim figure and a big bust and I always dress well. I was twenty-four when I met Steve...

"He keeps looking at you," Claire said, and I knew she was jealous. Well, to be honest, she wasn't in my league, looks wise, and I tended to be the one that men honed in on.

"He's giving me the creeps," I said. As I say he was not my type at all; he just wasn't good-looking enough and his clothes, which I guessed were actually quite expensive, had that scruffy, un-ironed look, which though fashionable with some, doesn't float my boat.

Even so, the next time we wanted a drink Claire persuaded me to go to the bar. Steve had his back to me and was talking to friends, and appeared not to notice me rise out of my chair and walk to the bar in my high heels. He did of course. I knew he was watching me - furtively.

I ordered more drinks and the barman placed the two large glasses of red on the bar, then before I could get my purse out of my handbag Steve was waving a tenner at the barman, but he wasn't looking at him or me - he was just casually leaning on the bar, ten-pound note in hand, talking, ignoring me, ignoring the barman. The barman looked at the side of Steve's head and then at me and I just shrugged and smiled. What's a free drink at the end of the day?

"Thanks," I said to Steve's back. He didn't reply.

Later, when his friends had left, he came over to our table and pulled out a chair.

"Mind if I join you?" he said as he sat down. Well, it was hard to say no after his generosity. We started chatting. He was charming. He was thirty-two and worked in IT. He was very disparaging, calling himself a geek. At the end of the night he asked for my number, but I was reluctant to give it to him as I didn't just date any Tom, Dick or Steve. I was more discerning. And anyway, there was something about him that did not quite add up. I made my excuses and popped to the ladies. However Claire, ever the matchmaker, told him what my number was when I was in the toilet - well, what are friends for?

"What's wrong with one date? You can always ditch him if he's not up to your normal high standard," Claire said sarcastically afterwards.

So it began. Our relationship. I lived at home with my mum and dad and Steve had an immaculate penthouse flat - whatever he did in computers it paid a lot of money. He was single, no kids, never been married though he had lived with a girl called Karen. He didn't say much about his past, in fact, he didn't say much at all. He was very quiet, and he didn't drink much. He was always in control - control was something Steve liked. He was just so different from my normal boyfriends; he had a flash car but he didn't drive fast, he had a gorgeous flat but it was tastefully decorated and modern, not a scruffy bachelor pad, he wore expensive designer clothes and took care of himself. OK, he was a bit of a techno freak but he didn't play computer games endlessly and he didn't have many friends.

I learnt all this, of course, as Steve collected me in the evenings and took me out for meals and to the theatre and the cinema. He told me I looked nice and asked me what I wanted to do. He was charming, a gentleman, and he didn't seem overly bothered about rushing me into bed either, which made a change. But I got the feeling he was holding something back; there was more to Steve than met the eye and I could not quite take to him.

Then, one day at his flat, I casually mentioned that I could not see him one Saturday as I was seeing Claire and some other friends. Steve's smile broadened.

"I don't think so, Brooklyn," he said. "You're my girlfriend now and I want to see you. You'll just having to text your friends and tell them you're seeing me and can't make it."

I was gobsmacked. "You don't own me. I want to see my friends," I said.

That smile never left Steve's face. "You're right, I don't. See your friends then and we split up."

"But that's blackmail."

"No, it's a choice Brooklyn. Have I not treated you well over this last month?"

I agreed he had.

"Have I not treated you like a princess and spent a load of money on you?"

Again I agreed he had.

"Well then, it's a small thing to ask. I was planning to cook you a meal next Saturday as you've not spent much time at my flat. I wanted it to be a surprise. If you're telling me you'd rather see your friends, then to me that means they're more important than me, and if they're more important then I'll be saying bye-bye. It's your call."

I couldn't believe it, but of course I texted them, told them I'd forgotten I was going out with Steve. They tried to reschedule, but what was the point? I knew Steve was not going to be happy if I saw my friends at any time.

I suppose, looking back, that was the start of it. The control. Steve took me to a lot of expensive places. I got to dress up loads and felt like a queen, but always there was that proprietorial arm around my waist or at my shoulder, and Steve never let me stray far from his side. I was very much his girlfriend. In some ways I liked it. I knew I was attractive and Steve liked showing me off. He didn't like sport or going down the pub with his mates or doing things normal guys did - as I say, he didn't have many friends. I was the centre of his life and I liked it. He bought me gifts all the time - perfume, jewellery, clothes - he paid for meals and, when we went out, we often shopped for clothes together and Steve would get his credit card out and pay whatever it cost. He was secretive about what he did in IT, and would not explain why he was so well paid and why he was sometimes away for days at a time "on a job". Still, he was my boyfriend and I loved him and I trusted him, especially after our first time in bed together at his flat; he was so loving and caring and tender.

But I knew he had another side. I'd seen it over seeing my friends and occasionally it came out when we had been out socially. He would look at me or kick me under the table if I so much as talked to or smiled at another man. Sometimes he would put me down by saying, "That's enough, Brooklyn." Or, "Brooklyn wouldn't understand that."

Then he would order for me in restaurants. He'd say I needed to lose weight as I had started to "pile on the pounds" since we'd started dating. Still, I enjoyed the meals, the theatre trips, the weekends away; it was a far cry from my usual boyfriends and the local pub or nightclub. I felt I had struck lucky with Steve - and Claire was oh so jealous. She told me how fortunate I was and how thankful I must be to her for having the foresight to give Steve my mobile number.

"You've always been too cautious with men," she said. "But this Steve is a really nice chap. You're great together. And he's loaded."

I suppose I knew I was a kind of trophy girlfriend. Steve liked me to look beautiful on his arm but didn't want me to say too much. Most of the time it was OK but sometimes it was annoying. I felt I couldn't speak. I couldn't be myself for fear of being put down or receiving a stern look.

I knew the tension was building up. One night he took me to a gala and I wore a silky black strapless knee length dress, which was quite figure-hugging. We had been dating for six months by that time. We went back to his penthouse and I lost my temper. I don't know why, it was just a pressure cooker effect. All the times I'd felt him watching me, judging me, telling me to do so and so. I just exploded. It was a tantrum and no mistake. I shouted. I screamed. I stamped my foot. And what did Steve do? Nothing. He sat in the armchair and watched as I had a right old go at him. He was totally unresponsive which was worse than him having a go back. In the end I picked up an ornament and threw it at him. It hit his forehead and bounced off and smashed on the floor. Blood began to trickle from his wounded head. That immediately calmed me down. I wanted to say sorry but couldn't find the words. My mouth felt dry.

Steve got up and walked casually to his bedroom and closed the door. I thought I had won. That Steve was going to bed. I felt in control. It didn't last. He came out of the bedroom. He had taken his jacket off and rolled up his shirtsleeves. In his hand he held a big, thick, leather belt which was doubled up. His face was red with rage. My heart beat rapidly. I knew I was for it. He had to chase me around the flat but when he caught me... well he walloped me... on my back and backside. The leather belt cut into me dozens of times. Whack! Wallop! Crack! And the worst thing of all was he didn't say a word. Not a word.

I lay on the sofa crying for ages, and then got up and went to the bathroom and cleaned off my make-up. I began to think perhaps I'd started it, because Steve actually hadn't said anything negative to me at all that night. Plus, I guess, in a strange way I felt erotically charged, I had provoked Steve and he had responded. I slipped into a silky nightdress, sprayed on some perfume and went to the bedroom. I slipped into bed. I knew I wouldn't sleep. Soon Steve was reaching over to me.

"I'm sorry, Babe, I didn't mean to hurt you but after you threw that ornament at me... well a red mist descended."

I told him I was sorry too and we started to kiss, gently at first but soon our tongues were entwining and we were snogging and pawing each other, and he had me on my sore back and his cock was up and so was my nightdress, and we were making love so passionately we both exploded within seconds.

I'm not sure how many times we made love that night... five? Six? Seven? We didn't get up until midday. Steve made me breakfast and took me home in the afternoon. Incident forgotten. That was the agreement.

But it wasn't. When I sat on my chair at work and looked at my computer my bum and back still felt sore, and was a constant reminder that I had been punished. Steve sent me flowers and chocolates and a card, and when I saw him I told him not to worry because it was partly my fault. He agreed.

"I just can't understand why you turned on me like that. It was so out of character," he questioned.

"We agreed to forget it, remember?" I said. I felt embarrassed by my part in the incident.

"Yeah, sure, let's not talk about it... the sex was good though," he said, and winked.

It was good and it got better. That image of Steve with the belt in his hand chasing me into the kitchen where he had finally cornered me filled my dreams. During the week, when I wasn't seeing him, I found myself masturbating over the incident.

Then, one day, we went out with some of his clients. For some reason I was feeling pretty chatty and nattered away to the wife of one of his colleagues. She had asked me about our relationship and I was honest in my answers.

The following day Steve and I went to a country pub for a drink, then as we walked back to the car he said, "I could have walloped you last night, big mouth."

"Why?" I asked.

"Telling Ingrid all that personal stuff."

I hadn't realised he'd been listening! "I'm sorry," I said, but from then on rather than just kicking me under the table or giving me the evil eye, he would whisper threats to me, like, "You wait till I get you home." Or, "You deserve a good spanking." Or, "Do you want me to use my belt again?"

It was subtle. Mind control. It went on for a while. Then one evening we got back from a meal out and he told me to bend over a chair.

"Why?" I asked indignantly.

"Because you've not behaved well the last few times I've taken you out. I've tried to warn you. I've been tolerant in the hope you'll change your ways, but you've not heeded the signals and now I'm going to have to punish you."

He pulled out a heavy dining room chair and told me to bend over the back and hold the seat. He went to the bedroom and came back with his belt. He unzipped my skirt and pulled my knickers down.

"Not on my bare bottom," I protested.

"Yes, on your bare bottom."

He lashed the belt through the air a few times to get me used to the snapping sound it made and to make me quake in my high-heeled shoes. He spread my legs apart and brought the belt down across my buttocks with a mind-numbing crack. And another. And another. The pain was unbelievable, it seared through my body. A fourth crack of the belt thrashed my upper legs.

I sobbed. "No more Steve, no more."

Tears fell onto the soft white cushion of the chair. Steve didn't reply. Instead the belt was swept down again and again. The searing heat pulsed though my bum cheeks and pulsated through my body. I gripped the edge of the seat as tight as I possibly could. I could not move. My feet felt rooted to the spot. Again Steve belted me. And again. I flinched. I sobbed. I begged.

Then all was still. All was quiet.

"I'm sorry, Brooklyn, I had to do it. Go to the bathroom and clean up and put your nightie on, and I'll pour some wine."

A thousand things went through my head. I didn't want any wine! I didn't want to be treated like a child and told what to do! A thousand things went through my mind but I did not say one word of them. Not one word. Instead, I stepped out of my skirt and ran to the bathroom, blubbing like a baby.

When I sat down next to Steve on the sofa and he ran his hands over my silky negligee I felt so aroused. The pain was still throbbing but there was a not unpleasant warmth to it as well. I mentioned how uncomfortable it was to sit down.

"Maybe you'd be better off lying down," he said, and led me to bed. The love we made was more intense than the first time.

That began a pattern. I suppose I had entered a BDSM relationship by the back door and I'm not sure how much Steve really knew about it either. But when we went out I knew I had to do as I was told. If I didn't I was liable to get punished by way of the belt or, sometimes, he would use his slipper.

One time we were at my parents' house and Steve and I were in their kitchen showing some holiday snaps. One was of me topless on the beach. I didn't really want dad to see it so I pulled it out of Steve's hand.

"Don't show that one," I said as the picture tore in half.

Steve responded with a sharp slap. It was a reaction rather than premeditated, and as I'd been slapped before I wasn't surprised. Dad was though, and didn't know what to say. Steve quickly apologised and I said it didn't matter and there were red faces all round.

A few days later I went shopping with mum and over coffee she asked, "Does he hit you, dear?"

"No, of course not," I lied. We both knew otherwise, of course. That slap had just been too instinctive.

They didn't say anything when I moved out though. Steve kept asking me to move in with him and I kept putting him off, telling him we were fine as we were.

"I'm beginning to think you've got another boyfriend," he would say.

"How would I have time to see someone else?"

"You've thought about it then, seeing another guy, and trying to fob me off."

That was Steve all over; always thinking I wanted to cheat on him. Possessive, jealous, and I guess that was why I was reluctant to move in. I consulted with Claire.

"Steve's nice, you should hook up together. He buys you sooo much Brooklyn and I'm sooo jealous."

We both knew I had little choice and that eventually he was going to give me an ultimatum and I would have to make a decision. He did it New Year's Eve. We were at my parents' house for a party, and just after the strikes of Big Ben had faded Steve dropped to his knee and asked me to marry him in front of the whole family. What could I say?

"It's stupid, you being in your parents' house when you're my fiancée," he said later.

And it was, so I moved in. He became more controlling then. He made me cook and iron and would inspect the flat to make sure it was up to his high stand of cleanliness. I swear he had OCD. I was always a little wary of him and would look around the flat anxiously before he came home from work to make sure it was to his liking. Of course I worked too but I got in earlier, and as I say, at times Steve was gone for days at a time on business. I suppose, like many women, the housework side just fell to me. Before my arrival Steve had employed a cleaner, but once I moved in I said there was no need and we could share the housework, which inevitably meant me doing it. Then there was the cooking. Although Steve was quite good in the kitchen he would only cook for friends at dinner parties, and because I was the first home from work well, I just put the dinner on.

The belt came out more frequently too. I guess there was more room for me to make mistakes once we were living together, and though it was painful the making up and lovemaking afterwards always put a spring in my step the next day. It was just something I had to live with.

One time we went to see Claire, who had moved in with her new boyfriend. I was rarely allowed to see my own friends but Steve made an exception with Claire. I think because I'd told him she had urged me to date him and then move in with him; he knew she was an ally. Anyway, we went around for dinner and afterwards I sat on Steve's knee as he and Mark talked about politics or something equally boring. Steve always liked me to sit on his knee. Claire and I made eyes at each other and as we'd both had a few glasses of vino I goaded Steve by making stupid comments. It's amazing how you start to act like a child if you are treated like one.

Claire encouraged my misbehaviour, which Steve ignored as he was having a serious debate with Mark who was of the opposite political view. Then, for reasons I can't explain, I started to unbutton Steve's shirt. Claire was laughing and egging me on. Eventually Mark realised as well and started to laugh. Steve put his hand on his chest and realised his shirt was no longer buttoned up, and knew his immature fiancée was responsible. He didn't say a word. Not a word. He gripped my arm and pulled me closer, twisting me round and pulling me over his knee. I could not believe what was happening.

"Not here!" I begged, suddenly feeling remarkably sober.

"Yes, here," he growled, and went to work belabouring the seat of my black cotton skirt while Mark and Claire looked on in amazement. It was a proper old-fashioned spanking, the like of which I'd not had since I was five. I felt embarrassed and humiliated. Clare and Mark did nothing of course. Afterwards Claire texted me to see if I was all right, but I'm sure she secretly enjoyed the spectacle. Bitch.

Worse was to follow, for we left shortly after and when Steve got me home the dreaded belt came out. He doubled it in two as usual, and as I took up my place over the back of the dining room chair Steve lashed my backside about twenty times on my bare bum. The pain was excruciating but the lovemaking made it all worthwhile.

And I suppose that's why I stayed. I didn't like the punishment but I enjoyed the making up part. That's what I told myself, though in reality I often felt wet when Steve was punishing me, and even when threatened with a walloping.

Still, as the wedding plans gathered pace, I was just not sure if I could spend my life with someone as controlling as Steve; someone who would not allow me my own friends and who liked to control every aspect of my life. He even chose clothes for me when we went out, or selected food off the menu for me when we went to restaurants.

I had a few days off work sick a couple of months before the wedding. I think it was stress. Anyway, on the third day I was feeling better, helped, I'm sure, by the fact that I had decided to leave Steve. After he had gone to work I packed my belongings into my car and drove to my parents. In the hall I put my arms around mum's neck.

"Mum, I can't go through with it - I can't marry Steve."

Dad started talking about how much had already been spent and he would not have me living back at home; they wanted to sell up and move to a bungalow. Mum was more compassionate and I went back to my old room. I expected Steve to call - of course he would call, but I was determined to be strong and not go back.

I drove in to work the next day, amazed he hadn't contacted me as I'd written him a long note explaining all my reasons for leaving him. I knew he would not take it lying down.

But he did. At the end of the second day he had still not contacted me. Each day I sat at work expecting a call or a text - but nothing. I was having to answer awkward questions too about my wedding plans. I said everything was going fine and even drove towards his flat each evening so colleagues would not know I'd left him. Days turned into weeks. I wondered what had happened to him, why he hadn't contacted me. I toyed with the idea that he had moved away, and even phoned his work to make sure he was still there, and hung up before I was put through.

"You'll have to find somewhere else to live, Brooklyn," dad said one evening over dinner. Your mum and I want to move now we're retired. I'm not rushing you - you know there's always a bed here for you, but if you have split up with Steve you need to find a place of your own."

A bed. That's all it was. A small bedroom. I realised how cramped it was and how I missed the mirrored wardrobes at Steve's house with all my designer clothes. And what would he have done with those? Cut them up? Sold them? I spoke to Claire, and she couldn't believe I'd left him.

"I knew he was controlling you but you had a great lifestyle with him."

"Can I come and live with you?"

"No way, Brooklyn," Claire said. "We've just not got the space."

So I lay in bed wondering if I had done the right thing, but most of all I wondered why Steve hadn't contacted me. I started to feel annoyed that he cared so little about me and he was going to let me go without a fight, which was the last thing I had expected. I couldn't sleep. I was depressed. I had more time off work. I got pills from the doctor. Dad wanted me to move out and kept dropping hints and even mum's compassion faltered. Also, having cooked my own meals - healthy options that Steve enjoyed - I was now back on mum's full fat diet. Not that I was putting on weight; I was slimmer than I had ever been. Worry. Stress. Anxiety. The best diet ever, ever.

I went back of course. I had too. Steve knew I would.

"I thought I'd give you a bit of time to clear your head... work things out for yourself... it's all been a bit intense and a bit rushed. I thought I'd give you space."

"But you never called, you never sent flowers, a letter."

"I wanted to give you space, Brooklyn."

Everything was how I had left it. All my lovely clothes were neatly hanging in the wardrobes... they brought tears to my eyes. Claire was right; so what if Steve was a bit of a control freak? He took me out for a meal to celebrate my homecoming, and he even bought me a new car. That was Steve.

"We'll have to put back the wedding," I told him in the restaurant.

"Why so?"

"We won't be ready in time."

He dabbed his lips with the napkin. "Don't worry, Brooklyn. Everything's in hand."

And it was! Steve organised the wedding completely, but I got to choose my own dress - a lovely white taffeta strapless affair. The wedding was wonderful and only Claire and my parents knew there had been a hitch. Pre-nuptial nerves, we called it. We got married in a church and, of course, I vowed to honour and obey and, after the reception, we went back to the flat. Of course Steve carried me over the threshold - he was very traditional like that.

"Look in the wardrobe," he said. "I've got a surprise for you."

I pulled back the mirrored doors to reveal the belt that had been used so often, but next to it was a paddle and next to that a cane and next to that a set of handcuffs. Steve put his arm into the wardrobe and pulled forth a dark object. It was long and thin and had a black leather handle. My heart missed a beat.

"Is that a whip?" I asked.

"Sure is. This," Steve said, "will be one of the few weddings that have started off with a thrashing. I think you deserve it after you ran off to mummy and daddy and left me with all the preparation, don't you?"

I was speechless.

Steve continued. "That's why I turned down the offer of the bridal suite in the hotel; up here no one can hear you scream."

He thrashed me then. With the whip. He ripped off my wedding dress and oh, dear God, did he thrash me!